FREEDOM RIDE

Colter reined south, gigging his horse again for good measure. People scattered in every direction and over the rush of the wind he heard startled shouts. As they thundered past the courthouse he caught a glimpse of the sheriff and Sam Lyons, and saw them claw at their guns.

The faint crackle sounded behind him like firecrackers, but suddenly a slug whizzed by so close he could hear it fry the air. Then a bolt of fire punched him in the side, spraying blood across his shirt, and he doubled forward over the saddlehorn. Ducking low, he glanced back just as Hungate swayed and toppled from his horse. The big man hit the ground flat on his back, slack and unmoving. Colter tasted something sour in his mouth, felt it rising in his throat, and he quickly looked away.

Then he was out of town and racing south. Toward No Man's Land. . . .

NOVELS BY MATT BRAUN

WYATT EARP
BLACK FOX
OUTLAW KINGDOM
LORDS OF THE LAND
CIMARRON JORDAN
BLOODY HAND
NOBLE OUTLAW
TEXAS EMPIRE
THE SAVAGE LAND
RIO HONDO
THE GAMBLERS
DOC HOLLIDAY
YOU KNOW MY NAME
THE BRANNOCKS
THE LAST STAND
RIO GRANDE
GENTLEMAN ROGUE
THE KINCAIDS
EL PASO
INDIAN TERRITORY
BLOODSPORT
SHADOW KILLERS
BUCK COLTER
KINCH RILEY
DEATHWALK
HICKOK & CODY
THE WILD ONES
HANGMAN'S CREEK
JURY OF SIX
THE SPOILERS
THE OVERLORDS

BUCK COLTER

MATT BRAUN

St. Martin's Paperbacks

This is a work of fiction. All of the characters, organizations, and events portrayed in this novel are either products of the author's imagination or are used fictitiously.

BUCK COLTER

For information address St. Martin's Press, 175 Fifth Avenue, New York, NY 10010.

ISBN: 978-0-312-97405-3

Printed in the United States of America

Signet edition / September 1989
St. Martin's Paperbacks edition / April 2000

St. Martin's Paperbacks are published by St. Martin's Press, 175 Fifth Avenue, New York, NY 10010.

10 9 8 7 6 5 4 3 2

To
That Ol' Gang of Mine
Cleo & Jim
Jerri & Barry
Sondra & Sumner

BUCK COLTER

ONE

The sun was bright as brass, warm and golden in a cloudless sky. Colter squinted against the early-morning glare and shifted in his saddle. The day was scarcely begun and already his throat felt like a dust funnel. He hawked and spat, and took a swipe at the brushy mustache covering his upper lip. His mouth was dry and gritty, as if stuffed with wads of cotton, and it came to him that spitting only made it worse. Sometimes he wished he had a taste for chewing tobacco—just to keep the juices flowing—but that was a case of the cure being worse than the ailment. Right about then he would have traded his left nut for a steamy cup of coffee, something to sluice the grime out of his innards. Still, dinnertime was a good three hours off, and until then he might as well crap in one hand and wish in the other. Aboard the hurricane deck of a cow pony it was strictly grin and bear it—and try not to swallow too often.

Stretched out before him was the Western

Trail, a snaky ribbon of churned earth connecting Texas with the railhead at Dodge City. Every spring, after the flood waters of the Red had receded, the cattle herds were pointed north across the grassy plains. Throughout summer and early fall the trail was clogged with an unending stream of bawling, cantankerous longhorns. While the herds were small, rarely numbering more than a couple of thousand head, sometimes ten or twelve outfits passed Colter's cabin between dawn and dusk. After fording the Red at Doan's Store, they plodded northward in a steady rivulet of horns and hooves and dust. Last year close to a quarter million beeves had shuffled past, and though spring had only recently transformed the tawny plains into an emerald sea of grass, herds were strung out as far as a man could see.

Colter and his partner, Emmet Hungate, rode for the XL, one of the largest spreads in No Man's Land. Their job was to inspect the passing herds and cut out any cows that belonged to the XL or its neighbors. It was a thankless task, long on sweat and short on sleep, but an accolade of sorts to their range savvy. While hardly more than full grown, they were old-timers in No Man's Land, and knew the brand of every outfit running cattle west of the line. The Trail crossed Beaver River where it flowed southeasterly into the Cherokee Strip, and it was here that they maintained a watch over the Texans. Cows that had drifted off home range and joined the trail herds were cut out and hazed back across the line. The Texans tolerated the practice, not out of honesty, or any sense of fair play, but because they couldn't afford trouble while trailing half-wild longhorns through a strange land.

The Cattlemen's Association had built a cabin along the trail, and from early spring to first frost Colter and Hungate called it home. Generally they were up at the crack of dawn, tending their small remuda and slapping together a hasty breakfast, and their day seldom ended much before the birds had gone to roost. But they were on their own for the most part—the XL foreman usually rode over once a week—and inspecting the Texas herds allowed them to escape the dubious joys of spring roundup. All things considered, it could have been a whole lot worse.

Especially for thirty a month and found.

That was a thought much on Buck Colter's mind these days. Thirty a month and found. A dollar a day, all the beans he could eat, and a sore butt to boot. It wasn't much of a bargain. Leastways not for a man who had notions of bettering himself. Most cowhands took to it like a pig in mud, and figured they had the world by the short hairs. But for him it was strictly a means to an end. A way station along the white man's road. The one he had chosen to follow for reasons all his own.

It was an old bone, yet one that Colter never tired of gnawing. He was just on the verge of working it over again when he spotted a Box T steer in among the herd. Straightening, he feathered his sorrel gelding lightly in the ribs and came down off a slight knoll. Emmet Hungate saw him coming but held his own position on the opposite side of the trail, just in case the steer broke the wrong way. Colter signaled the Texan riding flank, indicating with arm motions that he meant to enter the herd. The Texan waved back, bobbing his head, and Colter slowed the sorrel to a walk. Matching pace with the herd, he came in somewhat behind the Box T steer and began threading his way in and out among the longhorns.

Moving through a trail herd was ticklish business, dangerous to both horse and rider. Longhorns were easily spooked, vicious as a tiger when aroused, and perhaps the most aptly named of all the earth's creatures. Their horns often exceeded six feet in length, long curving blades that tapered down to razor-tipped points. They had been known to kill wolves and catamounts, and, on occasion, even a full-grown bear. What they could do to a cow pony, or a man, made an ugly sight. One that left little to bury.

Colter maneuvered his horse slowly, gently touching the reins only when absolutely necessary. The gelding knew his business at least as well as the man, and, in some instinctive communion between horse and rider, he even knew which steer they were after. Picking his way through the herd, mixing caution with boldness, the sorrel came up on the steer's off side, and they paced along awhile flank to flank. Then, in a series of scarcely discernible moves, horse and rider patiently crowded their quarry to the edge of the herd. There Colter popped the brute across the rump with his lariat and choused him toward a low swale of grassland near the river. Already some twenty cows were grazing along the tree-fringed bottoms, mixed brands from every outfit in No Man's Land, and the steer joined them like a wanderer home from an arduous journey.

Colter reined back toward the trail, softly making horse talk, praising the gelding for his deft performance. Again, the sorrel seemed to understand, and he gave a barrel-chested snort, prancing sideways in an arrogant little strut. The man grinned, amused by the horse's cocky response, yet at the same time proud to be astride his back. It was good, this thing they shared. A touching of spirits that white men never fully understood.

Yet, considering it further, he found the thought hardly surprising. There were many things white men failed to grasp. Perhaps, the more obvious a truth, the more difficult it was for them to accept. Certainly he had discovered that to be true in his own case. They looked at his tawny skin and high cheekbones, tied it together with the raven's-wing hair, and, quick as scat, they were ready to paste a label on him. Then they were suddenly caught up short, nailed by the pale gray eyes and the brushy mustache. Somehow, at that point it always fell apart, became a puzzle they couldn't quite piece together. It provided him with a certain detached amusement, watching their uncertainty kindle and take hold.

Failing to grasp the essential truth, puzzled by contrasts which defied quick explanation, they took the easy way out. Saw only what they wanted to see. Told themselves that their instincts were wrong and their judgments faultless. Not unlike a sleight-of-hand artist, he found it unnecessary to fool them, for they fooled themselves. It was simpler than he had suspected, this thing of the white man's road, and, in a queer sort of way, far more satisfying.

Colter grunted to himself, a smile playing at the corners of his mouth. *Ai!* It was a good game. One that few of the True People dared to play.

Suddenly he reined back sharply, setting the gelding on his haunches as Emmet Hungate loomed up before them. Lost in the shadows of his own thoughts, he hadn't been watching the herd. Even now the drag riders were hazing stragglers onward with curses and snapping quirts, and shortly the tail end of the herd would be across the Beaver. Clearly his talkative partner meant to make the most of the lull, before the next herd could arrive and block the trail.

Hungate slammed his pony to a halt in a flashy show of brute force. It was characteristic of him, something Colter had come to expect. He was a large man, heavy through the shoulders, and he liked big, mean horses that required rough handling. Yet he was a pleasant-looking fellow, with sandy hair and a square jaw, and the kind of wicked blue eyes that women found fascinating. They had partnered together for three years now, drifting into No Man's Land within days of each other. But Colter still found it puzzling that a man could understand women so well and horses so little. Gentleness was the secret to any creature's heart, women and horses most especially, but for some men it remained a mystery only half revealed.

"That was pretty slick, sport, whatcha did with that steer." Hungate gave him a crooked grin. "Tryin' to show them Texicans what a real cuttin' pony looks like?"

Colter shook his head and smiled. "Nope. That'd be sort of like teachin' the lame to walk and the blind to see."

"Gawddamn, just listen to him crow, wouldya! Quotin' bassackwards scripture like a drunk preacher. And me thinkin' you was a good upstandin' heathen the same as the rest of us."

"Why hell's bells, Em, after all this time I just figured you knew. I'm the heathenest heathen there is. Only trouble is, folks keep tryin' to convert me into an angel."

"Damned if that ain't the truth," Hungate cackled. " 'Specially a little towheaded filly with matrimony on her mind."

The big man's humor was infectious, and they both broke out laughing. But after a moment Colter's gaze drifted off to the distant herd, and a thoughtful frown came over his face. The drag riders were shouting and cursing stronger than ever, trying to force the stragglers into the river crossing. Hungate followed his eyes, then glanced back sharply.

"Buck, you got that look again. You ain't thinkin' what I think you're thinkin', are you?"

"Mebbe. Like the feller said, nothin' ventured, nothin' gained."

Colter gigged the sorrel and took off at a lope toward the river. Hungate watched after him in a quandary for just an instant, then shook his fist in the air and let go a throaty roar.

"You crazy gawddamned idjit! The Association's gonna skin your ass one of these days."

If Colter heard, he gave no indication, and moments later he pulled the gelding up alongside a Texan who seemed to be shouting louder than the others. He gave the man a businesslike nod and let a wooden expression creep over his face. The one he used for poker and horse trading.

"Howdy. You the ramrod of this outfit?"

"Most times." The Texan eyed him narrowly. "What can I do for you?"

"See you got some crips there." Colter jerked his thumb at a bunch of leppies and sore-footed yearlings that had shied off from entering the water. "Thought you might want to dicker on 'em."

Something changed about the Texan, and a crafty look came over his eyes. "Hadn't thought much about it one way or t'other. Why, you willin' to make an offer?"

"Likely they wouldn't make it to Dodge." Colter let his gaze drift over the bawling little knot of stragglers. "Fact is, they might not even make it over the river."

"Don't know as I'd say that," the Texan observed. " 'Course, they are slowin' me down a little bit. You make me a decent price and I might be willin' to let 'em go."

"I was thinkin' along the lines of four bits a head."

"Shit! That's good stock you're lookin' at, mister. Worth five bucks a head if they're worth a nickel."

"Dollar tops. Take it or leave it."

"God A'mighty, you oughta be robbin' banks."

Colter gathered his reins. "Been nice talkin' with you."

"Hold on now." The Texan groaned and mopped his face with a filthy kerchief. "Dollar it is. But I still say you're in the wrong damn business."

"Just write out a bill of sale and you can call me anything you like."

After the money had exchanged hands, Colter tipped his hat to the Texan and waved Hungate forward. They circled the stragglers from opposite directions and began driving them toward the grasslands south of the river. Hungate swung his horse over beside Colter and shot him an owlish scowl.

"Lemme tell you something, sport. You keep diggin' that hole deep enough and somebody's gonna bury you in it."

Colter grunted and flashed him a wide smile. "Hell, that's what it's all about, Em. The little dog diggin' up the big dog's bone."

TWO

After a dinner of warmed-over beans and bacon, and several cups of Arbuckle's best, Colter came outside to sit in the shade of the cabin. It was a good cabin, built of cedar logs with a thick sod roof and stone fireplace. Not as fancy as the one he was building for himself, but snug and comfortable nonetheless. Over the noon hour he had thought a good deal about that. The cabin. The piece of land farther up the Beaver. Settling down and raising a houseful of kids. Along with a herd of cattle, and a name that would one day amount to something throughout the territory.

That's what it was all about. To be somebody. Not just a raggedy-assed cowhand sweating his balls off for a dollar a day and beans. But somebody.

Leaning back against the cabin, he built himself a smoke and flicked a sulphurhead to life with his thumbnail. Puffing, he inhaled deeply, and let his eyes rove out over the land. Buying the stragglers that morning, adding to his small herd upriver, had set him to thinking about it again. It was a strong, rugged land. Tough and harsh, and yet bountiful for the man who could make his mark. Rolling plains covered with a lush carpet of graze. Watered by the Beaver and half a hundred creeks and twice that many natural springs. Well wooded along the lowlands and river banks, with timber enough for a man to build anything he had his heart set on.

A land big enough for any man. Where he could stretch himself. Better than most had, or would ever hope to find.

The Spaniards had called it *Cimarron*, which, loosely translated, meant "wild" and "unruly." Anyone who had ridden through it under a scorching summer sun or faced the polar blast of a plains blizzard needed no further explanation. In its own tenacious way it had defied both man and civilization. Through a hodgepodge of confused and poorly written treaties, it now belonged to no one. Yet there was nothing confusing about its borders. Texas and Kansas were separated by its depth of some thirty-five miles, while its breadth extended nearly two hundred miles from the Cherokee Strip to the Territory of New Mexico. It was an isolated expanse of rich grasslands and raw wilderness. Forgotten by God and government alike.

No Man's Land.

The Indians had used it first, as a passageway west during their fall hunts. Next came the renegades and outlaws, who turned it into a haven for murderers and thieves, beyond the reach of U.S. Marshals in Wichita and Fort Smith. Then, back in '76, when the Western Trail was opened to Dodge, it had come under the scrutiny of Texas cattlemen. What they saw fascinated them—an ocean of grass hundreds of miles closer to railhead than their own sparse lands. It wasn't Texas, but then, the vision of ambitious men was rarely limited by native sentiment. What intrigued them most was that no one—neither man nor state—claimed title to these vast rolling plains. It was free, open for grabs, and whatever a man was big enough to hold was there for the taking.

Less than seven years later some thirty ranches dotted the prairies sweeping north and south from the Beaver. Most were owned by Texans, but not a few had been bought by Scottish lairds and English noblemen. Towns sprang up along the river—Benton and Beaver City being the largest—and with time came a hardy breed of settler, hardscrabble farmers willing to brave fierce winters and the Godlike wrath of cattlemen in their search for roots and a home. While the squatters were as entitled to the land as the ranchers, the nearest law was five-days' ride to the east. Possession was what counted, the only title recognized, and what one man wanted he had to take and defend from another.

The ranchers were not long in uniting to protect their holdings. They met and organized the Western Cattlemen's Association, and over the past three years they had harassed the squatters with everything short of outright war. While there had been few killings, No Man's Land existed in a state of armed neutrality, and the situation grew worse daily. Settlers were pushing westward at an ever increasing pace, and now at last the cattlemen had their backs against the wall. Rather than yield another foot of ground, they would fight, and with the Association behind them, only the foolhardy seriously doubted the outcome.

Colter had seen the worst of it happen since the spring of '80, when he had drifted into No Man's Land from the Cherokee Strip. Yet, unlike most cowhands, he begrudged the squatters nothing. Their need for land—roots and a home—was an urge he understood. More than that, one he shared. When it came down to brass tacks, there was little difference between them. The settler wanted to plow the land, and he wanted merely to graze it. But to do so they would both have to challenge the Association. Which in the end meant a fight. On that score he had never fooled himself.

Hungate appeared in the doorway just as he finished his smoke. The big man squatted down beside him and pulled out a plug of Red Devil. He tore a chunk loose with his teeth and began working it into a manageable cud. When he had it mushed up properly, he shifted the wad to his off cheek and let go with a stream of dark brown juice. It splattered about six feet away, and they watched in silence as a little puff of dust rose and slowly settled back to earth. After spitting a couple more times, Hungate gave him a sideways glance.

"Y'know, I been tryin' to recollect if I ever come acrost anybody that had you beat for hard-headed. Near as I can figure, you got it won hands down."

Colter's mouth quirked in a smile. "Comin' from you, that's damn near a joke."

"Well, go right on and laugh your ass off. 'Cept while you're doing it, paste this in your hat. I ain't so bullheaded I can't see the writin' on the wall."

"Meanin'?"

"Meanin' just what I've said fifty zillion times since this mornin'. There's some folks that thinks you're gettin' too big for your britches. And I don't have to name no names. When they get wind you done bought yourself some more cows, they're gonna pitch a shit fit."

Hungate's way of looking at things was sort of gamy and unrefined, but he was no dimdot. Colter was forced to admit that he had a point. Among other things, the Association had passed a bylaw which forbade any cowhand to accumulate cattle of his own. Ostensibly it was a measure designed to stop the hands from burning their own brands on mavericks, but it went deeper than that, as everyone knew. The cattlemen simply wanted to eliminate all the competition they could, and they had started in their own backyard.

Colter grunted with disgust. "Sonovabitch, every time I think about it I get ticked off a little more. They tell us to slap the home brand on any slickear we come across—whoever it belongs to—and that's just peachy keen. But if a hand does it for himself they call it rustlin' and stretch his neck. Damned if that don't sound to me like the pot callin' the kettle black."

"Yeah, 'ceptin' for one thing. It's their game, and they're gonna deal the cards any way they see fit."

"That's where you're wrong, Em. I just signed on to ride for 'em, and part of the deal says I won't steal from 'em. But that don't make me their slave, and I'll be go to hell if it's gonna stop me from buyin' cows on my own hook. Nobody's big enough to stuff that down my throat."

Hungate regarded him dourly for a minute, working his cud over to the other cheek. "Buck, there's a whole lot of talk goin' around about old man Overton lettin' you build that cabin and set up between him and the Circle C. You don't hear it much 'cause you're such a standoffish bastard, nobody's got the gumption to tell you. But I'm tellin' you right now. When certain people hears you've been out buyin' more cows, they ain't gonna look the other way no more."

"Let 'em come. I've been cussed out before."

"Yeah, but they're liable to do more'n just cuss this time."

Again Colter had to admit that his partner was right. Still, he'd known that from the day he had made his deal with Ed Overton. Not that it wasn't a fair exchange. Overton wasn't getting any younger, and he needed someone to act as a buffer between him and the range hogs on his western boundary. The Association discouraged its members from setting the hired help up in business, and there weren't many hands around willing to tackle such odds. But Colter had accepted, demanding as his price a large chunk of land along Cottonwood Creek. Afterward he found Overton to be a strong supporter and a better friend, and the old man had helped him start his herd. While a year had passed and he still had fewer than a hundred head, it was a beginning. The first step on the white man's road. The second step was butting heads with the Association. It had to happen sometime, and the way things looked, it was about to become nose to nose.

He studied on it a moment longer, pulling reflectively at his ear. Finally he turned back to Hungate. "The way I see it, a man's only got two ways to go. He can bust his ass and eat beans the rest of his life, or he can get up off his haunches and try to make something of himself. To me, that's no choice at all."

Hungate was a little befuddled in the face of such massive calm. He blinked and made a couple of false starts before he got his tongue untracked. "Gawddamned if you ain't got me buffaloed. I could understand it if you was addled, but for a man that's got all his marbles to act the way you're actin' just don't make sense. Worse'n that, it's just plumb stupid."

"Yeah, it probably is. But I never was one to back off from a scrap. What with one thing and another, I don't reckon now's the time to start."

Hungate had no ready answer to that, for he knew it to be a fact. Buck Colter wasn't a big man—he stood slightly under six feet—but he was built along deceptive lines. Beneath his lean and wiry appearance was a frame thickly corded with muscle. He was fast and tricky and hard as nails. In the three years they had been together Hungate had never seen him pick an argument. Nor had he ever seen him lose a fight. Once Colter got hold of somebody, it was like chain lightning and a bag of wildcats all turned loose at the same time. Which was another reason most folks gave him plenty of elbow room.

Still, that didn't explain it all, and the more he mulled it over, the more Hungate began to see the light. There were some things a man wouldn't dream of doing for himself, and tangling with the Association was high on the list. But with a stiff pecker and his blood running hot, there was hardly nothing he wouldn't consider doing for a woman. Which brought it down to whose butter the fly had got himself stuck in. Rachel Goddard had an itch to get a wedding band around her finger, and Buck Colter was the fellow she'd picked to put it there. From the looks of things, it had been no contest. She had him thinking with his balls instead of his brains, and he was ready to take on the whole Association just to make an honest woman of her. None of which would bear repeating. Not out loud, anyway. And especially not to Colter's face.

The big man scratched his armpit and splattered the dusty earth with another squirt of tobacco juice. After a while he shuttled a glance over at Colter. "I just hope you know what you're lettin' yourself in for. You get them big poohbahs all riled up and they're gonna be like a bunch of burnt bears in a cave full of hornets."

"Funny thing about that." Colter chuckled

softly and started building himself another smoke. "Feller sees lots of stung bears along the way, but I don't never recollect seein' a squashed hornet. Sort of makes you stop and think, don't it?"

Hungate opened his mouth to say something, but nothing came out. At last his jaws clicked shut, and he gave his wad a furious gumming. Then, in a little flash of illumination, he understood why the words wouldn't come.

It had all been said.

THREE

Bloodgold shafts of light soaked into the cooling earth as the sun hovered on the far horizon. Twilight crept slowly across the burnished plains, and a soft breeze feathered the leaves on the cottonwood trees. It was the peaceful time of day, still and somehow hushed, when the earth paused to rest and all its creatures awaited the coming of night.

Colter was partial to evening, in the way a nighthawk comes alive with darkness, but just at the moment he had his hands full with other matters. Late that afternoon, shortly after the trail herds were driven to bed grounds for grazing, he had switched saddles from the sorrel to a dun gelding. Despite Hungate's mulish protests, he had then gathered his little bunch of scrubs and started them west along the old river trail. He meant to have them on his own land before nightfall, and with some hard riding he might even sneak in a visit to Rachel.

After skirting Benton he picked up the pace a

bit, hazing the cattle along with the nagging sense of urgency. Though the river trail was a public road, it made a beeline straight through Bar S land, and he was in no mood for explanations. People were just naturally suspicious of cows being driven at night, and if darkness fell before he crossed Timber Creek onto XL range, he might well be taken for a rustler. Once he hit the XL boundary, though, his worries were over. Alex McCord, the foreman, didn't approve of what he was doing, but he had never tried to stop him. Besides, he wouldn't be on XL land more than a mile, anyway. From there it was simply a matter of fording the river and chousing the scrubs onto Overton's Slash O spread. Then he could call it a night.

But even at that, it wasn't finished. More likely just begun. Hungate's warning earlier in the day had been the straight goods. The Association wasn't to be taken lightly. So far they hadn't given him a hard time, but that was no guarantee they wouldn't. Especially when word got around that he was back to buying cows off the Texas drovers. Unless he missed his guess, a whole bunch of people were about to start swelling up like dead toads in a hot sun. When they burst there was every likelihood that it would be him who got splattered.

Thinking on it, he was struck again by the white man's peculiar ways. Quirky, and sometimes downright absurd. Like this thing of the land. There was more than enough to go around, with some left over. In fact, out in the western reaches of the strip, there were hundreds of square miles populated by nothing but coyotes and outlaws. Yet that wouldn't do. Everybody was convinced that the choice graze was nearer the Western Trail—and the railhead at Dodge City. So they all bunched up, jostling and squabbling, in a thirty-mile belt along the Beaver.

Worse yet, they weren't satisfied with graze enough for a thousand head, or even ten thousand. Their greed for land seemingly knew no bounds. Like hogs starved for a mud wallow, there just wasn't enough dirt around to satisfy them. Overton's troubles with his neighbors—fellow Association members, at that—spoke eloquently of the white man's queer fixation with land.

Overton's eastern boundary was Clear Creek, and across it lay the Box T spread. Sim Hardesty owned the Box T, and as cattlemen went he wasn't a bad sort. Over the years he and Overton had locked horns a few times, yet Hardesty had never really made any concerted effort to poach on Slash O graze. Apparently he was content to live and let live, so long as nobody got ideas about his own fifty thousand acres. The same didn't hold true for Overton's neighbor on the west.

There the Slash O was bounded by Cottonwood Creek, and on the other side lay the Circle C. Unlike Sim Hardesty, the Circle C's owner had a real thirst for land, and his methods weren't exactly what they taught in Sunday school. Col. John Covington, formerly a military man, had delusions on a scale somewhat grander than most folks'. Already he was President of the

Cattlemen's Association, and controlled better than a hundred thousand acres between Cottonwood Creek and Beaver City. Part of the land he had settled himself, but a large chunk of it had been acquired from ranchers who couldn't match his ruthless tactics.

Covington paid his hands top dollar, and they followed his orders explicitly. Just in the last year he had made life so unbearable for the rancher on his southern boundary that the man simply pulled up stakes and trailed his herd back to Texas. The fact that his cattle had been stampeded regular as clockwork, while Circle C cows drifted farther and farther south, finally convinced him it was time to call it quits. Covington had watched him go, but then, still thirsting for land, turned his gaze eastward toward Cottonwood Creek. And Overton's Slash O.

Overton was a feisty old vinegaroon, though. While he wasn't as powerful in the Association as Covington, it took more than a few threats to make him roll over and play dead. Once the Circle C riders began harassing him, Overton went on the prod and started a search to find himself a stalking horse. It had ended with Colter, and their deal to lop off a hunk of land along Cottonwood Creek.

What none of them knew—neither Overton nor Hungate nor even Rachel—was that Colter had dealt himself a hand for reasons all his own. Col. John Covington was what had brought him to No Man's Land. And the chance to fight Covington—on a white man's terms—was what had prompted him to accept Ed Overton's offer.

Colter rarely thought about it any more. How it had started. Mostly he kept it tucked away in a private little cranny far back in his head. But sometimes, painful as it was, he let his mind slip back to those early years. When he had been a Cheyenne.

He was eight when it happened, and his name was An-zah-ti. Little Raven.

Like many squaws, his mother had been sold as wife to a white mountain man, who after one winter simply rode away and never returned. But behind he left his seed, and a few months later a boy was born. They called him Little Raven, for he had coal-black hair and strange gray eyes, and at the naming ceremony the medicine man ordained that he would one day become a great warrior. Which might have been true, except that the youngster never had a chance to fulfill the prophecy.

The Pony Soldiers came on a blustery winter morning when the People were huddled around fires in their lodges. There was no warning, no request for council, no attempt to identify the village as peaceful or hostile. The leader of the Pony Soldiers was concerned only that they were Indians—red heathens—and he attacked with orders to kill anything that walked. "Nits make lice" was the battle cry, and no quarter was granted women and children. That the slumbering village was led by Black Kettle, friend to all white men and the greatest peace chief of the Cheyenne, made no difference whatever. The only good Indian was a dead Indian, and the

Pony Soldiers gave them a benediction of fire and steel.

Before a warning could be sounded, the troopers came thundering through the village. Their sabers glinted in the pale wintry sunlight, and they hacked and slashed without impunity. Women and children scattered while the warriors formed to fight a delaying action. But it quickly became a slaughter, and for the Pony Soldiers it was little more than a gory new game, like chasing mice with sharp sticks. Their long knives turned the snow crimson with blood, lopping off heads and opening bellies that left bright fountains of life spurting in their wake. Only when their arms grew weary did they switch to guns, and it was then that Little Raven's mother was struck down.

She fell in the snow, her shoulder broken by a rifle slug, and with her last ounce of strength she pushed the boy over a shallow bank into the creek. Paralyzed with terror, the youngster cowered there and watched as a trooper leaped from his horse and began unbuttoning his pants. Little Raven's mother saw him also, and tried to crawl away. But the white man caught her, tore her dress off with a savage yank, and plunged himself between her legs. Grunting and thrusting, he drove her into the ground as his buttocks hammered and hammered and hammered again.

Just then the Pony Soldier leader rode up, tall and cadaverous, on a huge, fiery-eyed bay. "Hump it while it's hot," he shouted. "Give her hell, trooper!" Laughing, he wheeled his horse around and galloped back to the slaughter.

It was a face Little Raven never forgot.

Seared into the boy's mind was a picture of numbing horror: His mother shot down, then raped, and at last finished off with a pistol ball through the head. Yet these were thoughts he tried to outrun, to escape, as one would elude some unspeakable terror that comes in a dream. Instead, it was the face he wanted to remember. The face of the Pony Soldier leader.

Afterward there was a great outcry, and white men of conscience called it the Sand Creek Massacre. The Pony Soldier leader was relieved of command, driven into disgrace, and he disappeared from Colorado Territory. But there were many who called him hero, lauded his extermination of the savage heathen, and in time he again became a man of honor and stature.

Little Raven, along with other captured children, was sent to a Quaker missionary school outside Fort Sill. There he was taught the white man's way, encouraged to renounce the path of the True People, and instructed in the glories of the One God. While the passing of time in no way erased the massacre from his mind, the youngster slowly came to the realization that not all whites were barbarians. Much the same as with other races, the bad seed merely had a way of overshadowing the good. Yet, as he studied and listened and learned, one lesson stood out above all others: The red man was doomed to extinction unless he accepted the path laid out by the whites.

Some years later, grown to a strapping youth of eighteen, he put the reservation behind him.

Simply walked off in the dark of a spring night and never looked back. The Quakers had prepared him well, wiping out the guttural intonation from his speech and opening his mind to the customs of a world apart from his childhood. Though tawny-skinned, he easily passed himself off as white, growing a thick soup-strainer of a mustache to complete the disguise of his pale gray eyes. Still, a hidden part of him remained Cheyenne, and for reasons that seemed obscure to others, there was something strange and curiously different about him. Yet he was accepted as another fiddlefooted wanderer, one among an army of vagabonds, and found it ridiculously simple to weave a heart-rending tale of his orphaned past. Drifting into the Texas Panhandle, he worked his way up from horse wrangler to cowhand, and spent three years learning the ways of *wo-ha*—longhorns—the white man's buffalo.

Then, early in the spring of '80, shortly after turning twenty-one, he saw a name in the Fort Worth newspaper. Colonel John M. Covington. Covington, leader and guiding light of the Public Land Strip, had recently been instrumental in forming the Western Cattlemen's Association. Still using the name he had invented for himself, Colter quit his job and rode north toward No Man's Land.

Three years had passed while he waited and schemed and watched Covington rise to ever greater prominence. The cattlemen suspected him of nothing, yet behind Colter's every waking thought was the goad for revenge. Not an eye for an eye, but white man's justice. Some means, properly legal and above-board, of bringing about a final settlement of accounts.

Ed Overton had shown him the way, and given him the chance.

Colter shivered and slowly became aware of the night sounds. Darkness had fallen while his mind lived again in the past, and only when he heard himself muttering something in Cheyenne did he fully collect his wits. It was a temptation he had drilled himself to resist, this thing of summoning back all that had gone before. There was no need, nothing to be gained. The rage that lived inside him—gnawing at his bowels like a nest full of worms—was sufficient to the task. Dwelling on it would serve no purpose, for whatever hate man was capable of galvanizing was already his. A hundredfold and more.

Uncoiling his lariat, he spurred the gelding forward and began popping rumps. Moments later he drove the cattle through the shallow ford and onto Slash O range. Ahead, along the mouth of Cottonwood Creek, their journey would be done, and they could start filling their bellies on Colter grass.

It had been a good day's work. Calculated and neatly handled. Another slap in the chops for the Pony Soldier leader.

FOUR

Colter rode into the XL compound like a cat with a mouthful of feathers. Things were perking along at a good pace, just the way he'd planned, and he was thoroughly pleased with himself. Still, he felt obliged to have a talk with Alex McCord. The foreman had put up with a lot over the past year, and it didn't seem just exactly fair to let somebody start springing surprises on him. Like the new bunch of cows now grazing across the creek from Covington's spread.

Headquarters for the XL was a cluster of rambling log buildings: bunkhouse, stable, and corral, and the main house set back off by itself under a huge elm. Some Texan had slapped it all together in the spring of '77, but a couple of years back it had been bought by a wealthy Scotsman. A lord or laird, or whatever it was the gentry called themselves across the ocean. The man had set foot on the spread only once, the day he bought it, and then bustled off to wherever he'd come from. XL was strictly an investment, and, being a shrewd Scot who knew nothing about longhorns, he had hired Alex McCord to run the place. Though the new owner insisted on calling McCord his *manager*, the boys down in the bunkhouse still thought of him as the ramrod.

Fancy foreigners and their fancy ways were slow in catching on in No Man's Land. But that didn't stop them from investing in a good thing; there were at least a half dozen absentee owners who had bought land in the strip, mostly English noblemen who trimmed expenses to the bone and milked the spreads for fast profits. Which was something else that didn't set too well with the boys in the bunkhouse.

Colter found McCord at his desk in the big house, laboring over a set of account books. The foreman plainly welcomed the interruption, and shoved his chair back with a weary sigh. His face was windburned and seamed from a lifetime in the saddle, and he looked wholly out of place behind a desk. He stretched, loosening the kinks in his shoulders, and gave the younger man a rueful smile.

"Buck, lemme give you some free advice. Don't never let some slick talker cinch your ass to a chair. Christ, bustin' broncs is a regular picnic compared to sweatin' over these books."

Colter grunted and returned the smile. "Fat chance. They'd have to hogtie me and strap me down first."

"Just don't change your tune when your joints start creakin'." McCord dropped his pen on the desk and tilted the chair back on its hind legs.

"Howsomever, you don't ride in here to listen to me bellyache. What's on your mind?"

"Nothin' much. Just thought we might chew the fat."

"Horseapples. You're not one to waste your breath on talkin'. Them Texas drovers givin' you trouble? Or maybe Hungate's gone off on another toot."

"Nope. Everything's smooth and silky. No complaints."

McCord gave him a speculative look. "Which is by way of sayin' you've got some bad news for me. Well, go ahead and spit it out. I'm full growed."

"Wouldn't call it bad news exactly," Colter remarked. "Just figured you ought to know I drove twelve head over to Cottonwood Creek. Bought 'em from a trail outfit this mornin'."

"Jesus Pesus! I'd sure as hell hate to hear what you call good news."

Colter just stared at him, saying nothing. After a moment McCord slammed his chair to the floor and heaved another huge sigh.

"I'm not gonna beat my gums tellin' you what'll happen. I warned you last year when you started this monkey business, and things haven't changed none since. Not even a little bit."

"Why're you gettin' hot under the collar now? You knew about my deal with Overton right from scratch."

"Yeah, but goddammit, I thought you'd come to your senses. Mebbe go broke or something. The Association held off last year, thinkin' the same thing. But they won't no longer. Don't you see, Buck, they can't let you get away with it. Otherwise every cowhand in the strip would be runnin' his own brand."

Colter stiffened and bit down hard to hold himself in check. He felt like a small child rebuked for believing in the tooth fairy. All day long people had kept telling him his business, as if he didn't have sense enough to pour piss out of a boot. Yet anger was an indulgence he couldn't afford. Not yet. McCord was a fair man, but when it came down to the crunch, he owed his soul to the Association. Leveling with him now would be a damn-fool play. A one-way ticket to the boneyard.

"You want me to draw my time? I'd just as soon if this deal is gonna get you in dutch with Covington and his bunch."

McCord slumped forward, elbows on the desk. "Naw, hell, I know you need the money. Only thing I wish is that you'd gone to work for Overton to start with. Seems like he'd have wanted it that way."

"He did, but I backed off. If I was ridin' for him there wouldn't be no difference between Slash O and my own brand. This way I don't have to answer to nobody but myself."

"Independent as a hog on ice, aren't you? Well, I hope it's worth it, 'cause it's you that's gonna have to take the licks."

"I got a thick skin." He hesitated a moment, then turned to leave. "Guess I'll get on back to camp."

"Don't let the door hit you in the ass on the way out," McCord growled. "And the next time you've got any news, send me a letter. I'm gettin' too old for this shit."

Colter grinned, but he didn't look back. After he was gone Alex McCord sat staring at the ledgers for a long while. Somehow he wished he were twenty years younger and still full of piss and vinegar.

Instead of a flunkey bookkeeper for a tightfisted Scotsman.

Some two hours later Colter turned off the river trail and rode into the Goddard farm. Like most places where squatters were allowed to exist in peace, it wasn't much. A stretch of ground cattlemen either couldn't use or just didn't want. Most of the land along here was cut through by ravines that sloped down to the Beaver; during spring rains the whole farm turned into one big gully-washer. The only thing that saved the Goddards was a fifty-acre parcel of bottomland along the river. Silt and thick black loam had been washed downriver by a century of floods, and the earth was rich enough to grow rocks out of pebbles.

Goddard had it planted in cotton and an amazing variety of vegetables. That, along with his one milk cow and the occasional side of beef Colter brought by, was all that kept his family from starving. "Hardscrabble" was a word that had been coined especially for the likes of Joe Goddard. Yet his wretched efforts as a farmer were more than offset by his genius in bed.

He bred damned good-looking daughters.

Entering the house always made Colter feel

uncomfortable and out of place. Sort of bearlike. Goddard's wife and three girls had transformed the log dwelling into a regular emporium of female handiwork and dainty bric-a-brac. For a man accustomed to squishing around in cowshit, it was an intimidating, and not altogether rewarding, experience.

Rachel met him at the door with a wet kiss and a tight little squeeze. The younger girls, May and Bertha Lou, erupted in their usual fit of giggles, and the old man came forward to pump his hand. Goddard was a beefy, red-faced man on the sundown side of his forties. While he was a pleasant sort, always smiling and slapping everybody on the back, Colter suspected there was a method behind his cheery disposition. A man with three daughters just naturally had to win friends and influence people. Especially bachelors.

"C'mon in, Buck." Goddard grabbed his arm and all but jerked him into the parlor. "Take off your hat and stay awhile."

Rachel squeezed in beside him on a rickety settee, no more bashful than the rest of the Goddards. "I just knew you'd come callin' tonight. Bertha Lou said she saw you driving some cows up the road about dusk, and I told Ma, 'He'll be back. You just wait and see.' " She gave him a dazzling smile and nudged in a little closer. "And I was right. You're a sly devil. Buck Colter, but I'm on to your tricks. Did you buy us some more cows?"

"Uh-huh. Twelve head." Her whirlwind chatter never ceased to amaze him. Like a mockingbird she flitted from one subject to the next in the blink of an eye. But she was so cuddly and affectionate, that he gladly overlooked such a minor flaw. "Got 'em cheap, too."

"See there!" Rachel clapped her hands and darted a smug look at her sisters. "I told you so, didn't I? Someday he'll wind up owning this whole territory. You just mark my word."

The girls burst out giggling again, and after a second Bertha Lou simpered up with a coy smile. "Buck, you know what Rachel says? She says you're—"

"Awright, Sis! That'll do." The old man fixed her with a warning scowl. "You girls tend to your knittin' and quit pesterin' Buck."

Sarah Goddard stuck her head out of the kitchen and surveyed the girls with a frosty look before she glanced over at the settee. "Evenin', Buck. Can I get you some coffee? Or a piece of pie, maybe? It's fresh baked."

"No, ma'am. Thanks all the same. I've still got some ridin' to do if I'm gonna make it back to camp."

"Camp?" Goddard echoed. "Why shucks, boy, I thought we'd have ourselves a good talk. Gets kind o' lonesome around here listenin' to these four jaybirds jabber at one another. Near enough to drive a man to drink." Something flickered in his eyes. "Speakin' of which, I just happen—"

"Daddy, shame on you. It's me he came to see! Not that old jug of yours." Rachel bounced off the settee and pulled Colter to his feet. "Come on, sugar, let's go for a walk. I swear this family of mine thinks they're the ones that are engaged.

Now I want you to tell me all about those cows you bought. And what you've been doing on the house."

Joe Goddard pulled out his pipe as they went through the door. He broke tobacco off a dried twist and crushed the leaves in the palm of his hand. After he had the blackened bowl filled and lighted, a little smile crinkled the corners of his mouth. As if he were gloating about something. Perhaps even patting himself on the back for a change.

Rachel snuggled closer in his arms. They were stretched out on the grassy bank of a small creek some distance from the house. Overhead, silty beams of moonlight filtered through the leaves of a cottonwood, and the only sound was the chirping of crickets along the stream. It was their special place, off away from everything and everybody. Where they came to be alone and say things not meant to be overheard.

They lay together in a tangle of arms and legs, touching and kissing and mouthing little noises that had meaning only to themselves. Their breath grew shorter, coming faster, and across the stream the crickets went silent as Colter groaned deep in his chest. At last Rachel wiggled free, pushing him back. Not so far away, though, that she was out of reach.

"Lordy mercy, sugar, you just overpower a girl. I think maybe you shouldn't stay away so long. It makes you—" She giggled and tugged playfully at his mustache. "You know, like a bull when they turn him loose with the cows. That's what you are, just a big old hungry bull."

"You talk too much. Come on back here and kiss me some more."

"Well, I like that!" She tossed her head and gave him a sulky look. Little flecks of gold shimmered in her hair, and the pale light turned her eyes a curious shadowy blue. "You stay gone nearly a week and then all you want to do is squeeze me to death. Why, you haven't said a word about the house—not one word—and that's important. How'll we ever get married if we don't even have a house to live in?"

Colter's hand crept under her skirt and started up her leg.

"Buck, you stop that right now!" She shivered a little, but she didn't move away. "There's more important things than messin' around, and you know it very well."

His fingers reached her thigh and began stroking softly.

"Buck, don't." She moaned and edged a little closer. "We shouldn't."

"That's not what you said the first time."

"Sugar, I just melt when you touch me like that. I can't even think."

"Then quit tryin'."

He lifted her skirt, running his hand over the gentle swell of her hip. She whimpered and thrust herself under him, her lips parting as his mouth came down hard. There was a sharp intake of breath, and then in a low, trembling voice she began chanting his name over and over again.

The moon drifted behind a cloud, bathing

them in darkness, and a breeze rustled softly through the cottonwood. Across the stream the crickets listened and waited, their serenade forgotten.

FIVE

Late Saturday afternoon, Colter, leading a pack horse, rode into town for supplies. Emmet Hungate tagged along as far as Benton, then took off like a scalded cat along the river trail. Saturday night was Hungate's night to howl, and he had a new flame over in Beaver City, some twenty miles west. Watching him tear off down the road, Colter had to laugh. The big man had a boyish enthusiasm for women and whiskey and saloon brawls, in just about that order. Judging from past experience, Hungate would crawl into camp sometime Sunday morning with a massive hangover and a freshly skinned head.

Not that Colter faulted him. That's why most cowhands were content to remain cowhands. Because there were no strings attached. Footloose and fancy free. At liberty to see the elephant in whatever fashion suited the man, even if it killed him. Before meeting Rachel, Colter had been exactly the same way. Perhaps even wilder once he'd downed a load of popskull.

Now, though, he was a reformed man. Pillar of the community. Hadn't had a fight in close to a year, and hardly ever felt that old temptation to start sniffing saloon girls. Thinking about it, as he rode into Benton, it came to him that he hadn't even been drunk. Except for the time old man Goddard lured him out to the barn and got him ossified on white lightning.

Walking the straight and narrow. That's what it boiled down to if a man meant to get ahead. Yet the thought made him chuckle. In some ways, this business of settling down had its drawbacks. There was much to be said for brawling and whoring and swilling firewater. It was a good life, and not without certain advantages. Still, there was more to be said for Rachel. She had a way of making a man forget such things. And when she really put her mind to it, there wasn't anything short of a bolt of lightning that could run her a close race. She just naturally galvanized a fellow, and sometimes it was days afterward before his hair uncurled.

Suddenly he was anxious to get the supplies loaded and be gone. The Goddards were expecting him for supper, and afterward, when the moon came out, he'd likely get something extra special for dessert.

Colter hauled up in front of Savage's General Store and dismounted. The town appeared much as it always did on a Saturday afternoon, wagons crowding the street and the hitchracks lined with horses standing hipshot in the drowsy heat, women beating a steady path between the general store and Emerson's Mercantile, all gussied up in their starchy dresses and foofaraw, cowhands trooping into their favorite watering holes, or congregating outside to swap windies and ogle the ladies. All in all, it was pretty impressive. Considering the way it had started, Benton had come a long way.

Three years ago, when Colter first rode into town, the street had been little more than a wide hog wallow. There were only two buildings then, Dix's Saloon, on the side nearest the river, and, directly opposite it, the general store. The rest was virgin prairie, still strewn with scattered bones of the slaughtered buffalo herds. But early that summer—the first summer after the Association had been formed—Benton became something of a boomtown. Word got around that the cattlemen were there to stay, and the rush was on. Buildings sprang up on both sides of the street, wobbly structures that looked as if they had been slapped together with spit and poster glue. Overnight, or so it seemed to those watching, the town mushroomed into a bustling little community. Another saloon was added, the mercantile and Fenner's Hardware opened their doors, and Doc Chase hung out his shingle. Before summer was half gone Benton had a hotel, a livery stable, and its own weekly newspaper, the *Benton Banner*. That fall the first school in No Man's Land, a one-room sod affair out at the west end of town, began dispensing higher learning to the local small fry.

It had all happened at a dizzying pace, in a whirlwind period of three months, and the natives were justly proud of themselves. Beaver

City also came alive that summer, but it was farther west, and its growth seemed slow by comparison. People in Benton were fond of saying that their sister city wasn't so much a rival as a joke. Which bore an element of truth. Most cattlemen conducted their business where they always had, and left Beaver City to the sodbusters.

Colter felt much the same way, but not altogether for the same reasons. Towns tended to stifle him—a throwback to those early years with the Cheyenne—and he generally felt more at ease out on the plains. His fascination with Benton was not for the buildings or the people, but rather with the town's leading citizen. Curiously enough, though, his infrequent encounters with Covington were moments he had come to dread. Three years of waiting and planning had done nothing to lessen his hate. Like the temptation to bite down on a sore tooth, it was all he could do to resist shooting the man on sight.

Ironically, on a day when his thoughts dwelt more on Rachel than on revenge, he stumbled into Covington straight off. Ducking under the hitchrail, he raised up and saw the cattleman striding down the boardwalk toward him. Covington was headed for the Association office, which was jammed in between the hotel and Savage's Store, and he seemed preoccupied with some weighty matter. Just for an instant he failed to spot Colter; then he happened to glance up, and their eyes locked.

Covington was tall and thin and glacial. Even in a range coat there was something cadaverous about him, and his eyes were like dull agates stuck in an old and shrunken skull. There was something queer about him, a sense of mold and decay. As if he spent his nights among slimy things that had neither form nor name. But, for all his appearance, he was a vital man, and he knew how to hate. Particularly those who dared oppose his will. Though his eyes were flat and guarded now, there was no concealing what lay behind the look.

Colter's face was a bronze mask in which nothing moved. He had a tight grip on the rage bottled up inside him; allowing it to spill over now would accomplish nothing. A lifetime had passed between a bloody winter's morning on Sand Creek and a dusty town in No Man's Land. It had been a slow and painful journey, and along the way he had learned the virtue of patience. Much like a hunter stalking game, he steeled himself now to wait a while longer. Soon, in some way as yet unrevealed, he would provoke this man. Force him to break the law. The white man's law. Then he would kill him.

That day would come. In its own good time.

They stared at each other a moment longer, something silent and ominous passing between them. Then Covington turned and strode through the office door. Colter stared after him, sorry that it had ended so abruptly. A tiny muscle pulsed on his temple, and as he listened to its throb he slowly became aware of something else. Something new and curiously sweet.

He was enjoying this.

From now until the time he killed John Covington would be the happiest days of his life.

Gratifying and tantalizing and immensely rewarding to his heathen soul. A time of joy. More fulfilling than any he had ever known.

"Looks like the Colonel got the word."

The voice startled Colter out of his funk, and he turned to find Ed Overton standing in the entrance of Savage's Store. Clearly he had watched the scene with much relish, for a foxy grin was plastered across his face.

Colter stepped onto the boardwalk and walked forward. "What word is that, Ed?"

"Why, that you done bought yourself some more cows. What else?"

"Word does spread fast. How'd you find out?"

"Same way Covington did, I reckon. One of my line riders spotted some new brands runnin' with your bunch. Don't take much horse sense to figure where you got 'em."

"No, I guess not. Way you're grinnin', I'd judge you sorta like the idea."

"Damn right!" Overton chortled. "I like to see a young feller get ahead in the world."

The old man's crafty manner was wholly in character. Short and chunky, built for comfort rather than speed, he had lived by his wits most of his life. White-thatched now, with a snowy mustache, he resembled some venerable sage that had been sent out to dispense wisdom across the land. His face had the cured look of weathered saddle leather, as if he'd been dipped in a tanning vat and left to soak way past his prime. But every wrinkle had been gained through bitter experience, and, like an old graying wolf, he had long since mastered the tricks essential to survival.

Colter recognized him for the slippery devil he was, but that in no way lessened his admiration of the old man. Overton made no bones about what he was or what he'd done. Their deal put a wall of sorts between himself and Covington, and he'd been blunt about it from the outset. Anyone who wanted to risk it might get rich. Or, then again, he might get dead. Strictly a roll of the dice. Colter could understand a man like that. Outspoken, shrewd, and brassy as a bulldog. It was a rare combination.

Overton took a swipe at his mustache and glanced around to see if anyone was within earshot. Satisfied, he motioned the younger man out of the doorway and lowered his voice. "Just between us, I got another little deal brewin'. If it works out, you might be bossin' your own spread sooner'n you thought."

"Yeah. What's that?"

"Never you mind what's that." Overton gave him a cagey look. "When she pops I'll be around. Meantime I just wanted you to know I was thinkin' about you."

Colter couldn't resist a grin. "Naturally, there'd be something in it for you."

"Why, Christ, yes! You don't think my pappy raised any dimwits, do you?"

Chuckling to himself, Overton ambled off down the street. Colter stared after him a moment, scratching his head over the cryptic offer. Then he gave it up. The old man had more dodges than a medicine-show pitchman. Trying to second-guess him was about like spitting into the wind.

Colter started toward the store, but then he stopped. All of a sudden he felt like a drink. One quick shot to celebrate putting a burr under Covington's saddle. Then he'd load up with supplies and make tracks for Rachel's place. Turning, he tipped his hat to a couple of starchy little ladies and headed back the way he'd come.

Moments later he pushed through the doors of the Yellow Snake Saloon and made a beeline for the bar. The place was doing a lively business, packed with cowhands from every outfit in the strip. Evidently they'd gotten an early start, and from the looks of things it would wind up a real interesting Saturday night. After the barkeep poured him a shot of the good stuff, he bellied up and began sipping it slowly. One was the limit he'd put on himself, but there was no reason he couldn't stretch it out.

Somewhere around his third or fourth sip, a hand from the Circle C pushed in beside him and slapped the bar for service. Colter had seen him around but couldn't place his name. The fellow was tall and thick-shouldered, with a square, brutish face, and his mood seemed to match his looks. He ordered the bartender to leave the bottle, and knocked back two quick shots with hardly a pause for breath.

About then Colter got a funny feeling down in the pit of his stomach. Some instinctive nudge that things weren't as they seemed. But the reaction came a moment too late. The cowhand poured a third drink, then faked a sideways stumble, slamming into Colter, and sloshed whiskey across the bar.

"Clumsy sonovabitch!" He whirled around. "Look what you done. Spilled my drink."

Colter took a step away from the bar. "Friend, I'm not lookin' for trouble. Why don't you have one on me and we'll call it quits?"

"The hell you say!"

Setting himself, the cowhand launched a looping haymaker that would have demolished a stone privy. But it landed in an empty little pocket of air. Colter seemed to be fading backward, away from the punch, but suddenly his foot lashed out in a sideways kick. Boot and kneecap came together with a sickening crack, and the man let go with a pitiful scream. His leg buckled under him, and he started down.

Colter moved in swiftly, dropping low, and delivered a crushing blow to the sternum bone of the chest. The cowhand shuddered, suspended in motion for a mere instant, then toppled forward like a felled ox. Froth bubbled out of his mouth, and his leg twitched. Then he lay still.

Glancing around the room, Colter ruefully shook his head. "Somebody ought to teach that peckerhead to pick on people his own size."

Wheeling about, he casually strolled out of the saloon. When he went through the door, he was grinning and whistling a tuneless little ditty under his breath.

Ai! The opening gun had been fired.

SIX

John Covington stared at a fly speck on the office wall, almost as if he had gone to sleep with his eyes open. He was a man given to frequent moods of introspection, more comfortable with his own thoughts than with other people. While he understood what made them tick, it was with the detached curiosity of a coroner performing an autopsy. Not unlike lizards and other cold-blooded creatures, he was without tolerance for the weaknesses of his fellow man.

Just at the moment he had withdrawn inside himself and was examining one Buck Colter. It was a process he often employed, sort of a mental dissection. Somewhere in the nether reaches of his mind he slowly and very painstakingly carved the other man into little pieces. Once the puzzle had been disjointed, he held each part to the light and carefully scrutinized it. Time and motion were arrested, lost all meaning, while he studied the problem. His mind's eye focused solely on motive and intent—the impulse behind

Colter's actions—and, like a scientist probing the entrails of a frog, he examined each piece for some hidden clue.

Though Covington's impersonal manner gave most men the shudders; he was not so cold and unfeeling as he appeared. Time and events had eroded the gentler aspects of his nature and left revealed only the hard and dispassionate core of his inner self. Nearly two decades past, shortly after the Civil War, he had come west seeking a new life. Along with thousands of others who had survived the bloodbath, he sought fame and fortune not so much as a fresh start. The chance to build and grow and reap the bounty of a generous earth for himself and his family.

Yet what he found was something other than what he sought. With his wife and son he settled on the high plains of eastern Colorado. There he built a small house, began buying cattle, and set about making his mark on the land. That first summer was a peaceful time of immense progress, and while the winter was brutal and unrelenting, the hardships in no way tarnished his outlook for the future. Next spring his wife gave birth to a tiny girl, whose soft gurgling and sunny disposition made him an instant slave. Looking about him, he saw the provident hand of God at work, gracing his life with health and love and freedom from want. He was content, a man blessed by his Maker.

Then, in a single afternoon, his world shattered. Returning from Julesburg with supplies, he found his house burned to the ground. Near the corral his small son had been axed and scalped, and the baby girl spitted on a sharpened stake. Blinded by tears, gagging on his own vomit, he stumbled away, only to discover the final horror in a patch of weeds behind the house. There his wife had been stripped naked, assaulted until her womanhood was a gaping wound, and then killed. Her throat had been cut from jawbone to jawbone, and her features had slipped down in the rubbery, distorted mask of those who have been scalped.

Only the flies sang a hymn to his dead, and it was a sound he never forgot.

Afterward he learned that a war party of Northern Cheyenne had swooped down across the plains, burning and pillaging and raping in a murderous orgy of bloodletting. That other settlers had suffered a similar fate did nothing to blunt his own grief. He became something of a fanatic, fiery-eyed and riddled with hate, obsessed with bringing the retribution of the Lord God Jehovah to the heathen savage. Over the next year he acquired a following of sorts, and the Governor was persuaded to commission him a colonel in the territorial militia. Winter brought him the command of a mounted brigade, and along the banks of Sand Creek he led a slaughter no less inhuman than those of the painted hostiles.

That the heathens he punished were Southern Cheyenne, living at peace with the white man, made no difference to him then or afterward. He had visited the wrath of God on the savage horde, and with it came some measure of comfort from the thing which gnawed at his bowels.

The years that followed were neither unkind nor rewarding. Driven from Colorado in disgrace, he crossed the great mountains into Oregon. There he found both the land and the people wanting, and in time he drifted southward into California. But warm ocean breezes and balmy nights weren't to his liking either. Ultimately he found his way to Tombstone, staking a claim early on in the strike, and sold out for a modest fortune when the large mining companies moved in to take over. With wealth and the passing of time, the stigma of Sand Creek no longer dogged his tracks. He again became a man of stature, respected and sought out for his advice, and it was generally agreed that, after all, he had performed a service for his country. Custer on the Little Big Horn had proved beyond question that there was only one solution. If the white man was to live in peace, then the savages must be driven onto reservations, or, better still, exterminated. Just as John Covington had done at Sand Creek.

Yet, for all his money and prominence, Covington remained a disgruntled man. The long journey to the Pacific shores and back again had brought him fortune and restored his name, but with it came only a modicum of peace. Somehow he yearned for the vast plains, where the wind blew free and the grass rippled green and velvety beneath a golden sun.

Where he had once been graced with all he sought.

Less than a year later he appeared in No Man's Land, trailing a herd of cattle and armed with letters of credit from the largest bank in Fort Worth. The land was free for the taking, and those who had arrived before him gladly made room for a man of such obvious influence and power. The strip needed men of his caliber if it was to prosper and grow, and they counted themselves fortunate that he had chosen to cast his lot in a raw, untamed wilderness. After scouting the land thoroughly, he selected range west of Cottonwood Creek and set about arranging the order of things to suit himself.

Covington's methods were harsh by any yardstick, and, in the eyes of some, wholly lacking in scruples. Still, he saw himself as neither evil nor greedy. Life had taught him that only the strong endured. The meek inherited nothing more than six feet of sod and a wooden marker. Through nearly two decades of wandering—from the high plains of Colorado to the silver lode of Tombstone—he had learned one essential truth: Money and power were tools, like a spade or an axe, to be used in carving out whatever niche a man coveted most. Only fools and weaklings failed to recognize this most elemental of all tenets.

Shaped by the vicissitudes of life, he had become an unyielding pragmatist. For him, the means justified the end, and any qualms he might once have possessed had long since been submerged beneath a shell of godlike righteousness.

That imposing temper was centered just now on Buck Colter. Try as he might, Covington couldn't come to grips with the riddle. From what he knew of the man, Colter was hardly a fool. Nor was he some gullible young greenhorn to be taken in by Ed Overton's devious sleight of hand. Clearly he knew what was at stake—both the Association and the Circle C would move to stop him—and yet he appeared heedless of the risks. All of which troubled Covington in a way that left him vaguely uneasy. David and Goliath was an enduring fable, but in real life things simply didn't happen that way. Any man who willfully provoked the Association was not a man to be trusted. There was something more to him—and his lone-wolf operation—than met the eye.

Covington had an abiding dislike for enigmas, particularly those which defied all the rules of logic. There was something shrouded and obscured about Colter, some part not yet revealed. As the cattleman mentally fitted the pieces back together, once again forming an image of the whole man, he remained distinctly aware that some vital part had been overlooked. The missing link.

The door flew open, and Wash Sealy, the Circle C foreman, burst into the office. Covington jerked awake, startled out of his ruminations, and gave Sealy a blistering frown.

"Wash, you know better than that. I've told you before to knock before you come through a door."

"Sorry, Colonel. I was sorta in a hurry and it just slipped—"

"What's the matter with you, anyway? You look like you've seen a ghost."

Sealy shook his head, slinging pellets of sweat across the room. "Not unless spooks come in flesh and blood, I ain't. Colonel, I don't know exactly how to tell you this, but that Colter kid just beat the livin' crap out of Buster Culpepper."

"Culpepper?" The cattleman's brow screwed up in a quizzical frown. "Wash, what the Sam Hill are you talking about?"

"That's what I'm tryin' to tell you. Buster picked a fight with Colter, and the bastard just ate him alive. Snapped his knee right at the joint and hit him some funny kind o' way in the chest that's got him spittin' blood like a stuck hog. Happened not five minutes ago, right over in the Yellow Snake."

Covington eyed him narrowly. "Why would Culpepper pick a fight with Colter?"

The foreman shrugged, and a sheepish smile nudged the corners of his mouth. "Well, it was my fault, I guess. I put Buster up to it. Figured we'd give Colter a little warnin', only it didn't work out that way. Goddamn, Colonel, you ain't never seen nothin' like it. He just gobbled Buster up and spit him out in pieces."

"Quit ranting about Culpepper. What I want to know is why you sicced him on Colter."

"Why, y'know. 'Cause he's been buyin' cows. I thought—"

"You're not paid to think! Or hasn't that message gotten through to you yet? You're paid to take orders. Nothing more."

"Yeah, but hell, Colonel, you said yourself he was settin' a bad example for the rest of the hands. Damnation, if he ain't stopped ever' saddletramp in the strip is gonna be startin' up his own outfit."

"You're absolutely right, Wash. I did say that." Covington straightened in his chair, cold and remote as a sliver of ice. "But I didn't say anything about having him whipped. Now let's understand each other. I'm giving the orders around here, and until I say different, I don't want Colter touched."

"Don't want him touched?"

"You heard me. There's something queer about this whole deal, and until I find out what's behind it, he's to be left strictly alone. Him *and* his cows."

"God A'mighty, Colonel." Sealy threw up his hands helplessly. "You leave him go off on his own hook and there's no tellin' where it'll wind up."

"That remains to be seen, but the order stands. If we did anything now, chances are we'd just turn him into an underdog of some sort. Which might be more dangerous than letting him run a few cows."

"You mean the hands are liable to get the idea he's somethin' on a stick and start choosin' up sides."

"That's precisely what I mean. And it might well be that he's trying to goad us into a fight for just that reason." Covington settled back in his chair, calmer now, and a pensive look came over his face. "No, we'll let Mr. Colter fry in his own fat for a while. The Association is due to meet the first of the month, and by then it's entirely likely he'll have tipped his hand."

"What you're sayin' is, give him enough rope and he might hang himself."

"Could be. We'll just have to wait and see. However it falls, though, I want it to be the Association that handles it and not the Circle C. That way nobody can point the finger at us when it's over and done with."

"Meantime, we just act like he ain't there." Sealy chuckled softly. "Colonel, I got to hand it to you. That's damn smart thinkin'."

"Glad you approve, Wash. Now quit wasting time and go see if Ed Overton's still in town. Tell him I'd like to have a talk if he can spare me a couple of minutes."

"Overton?"

"That's right. We'll give Colter plenty of slack for the time being, but it occurs to me we might draw the knot a little tighter on Overton. The man that has the most to lose sometimes has the least backbone."

After the foreman left, Covington leaned back in his chair and focused once again on the fly speck. Slowly, with the deft and certain strokes of a surgeon, he began to dissect Ed Overton.

SEVEN

High overhead a hawk floated lazily against a gritty bronze sky. Colter paused, shielding his eyes with his hand, and watched for a moment. Then the hawk caught an updraft, climbing higher still, and vanished in a golden streamer of light. Smiling, he pulled a kerchief from his pocket. *Ai!* It was as the old ones had said in his youth. A hawk in the sun was a good sign. Fair days and full bellies to come. He mopped his face, savoring the taste of clean, salty sweat, and went back to work.

The cabin site was on a small knoll, overlooking a horseshoe bend in the creek. Cottonwoods towered above the clearing on all sides, and the mewling ripple of the stream drifted in on a soft breeze. There was a tranquility about this spot that appealed greatly to Colter. Wild things came here to water, marking their passage with tracks along the bank, and overhead the trees were alive with birds. The cheery call of the meadowlark and the bobwhite blended as one farther back from the creek, and hummmgbirds flitted in bright green flashes among the prairie flowers.

The first time he saw the bend he knew that this was where he would build, below the crest of the knoll, on a broad curving shelf, where the house would be shaded in the summer and sheltered in the winter. But practical considerations were only a part of it, and a small part at that. He had selected the spot for what it was rather than what it might become, and he meant to leave it unspoiled and free of blemish. After the cabin and a corral were raised, nothing more would be built along this stretch of the creek. It would remain as he had first seen it, and here he would find again the harmony of self he had known as a boy along another stream.

A oneness with the earth and its creatures and the sacred winds.

Thinking about it now—the hawk, the peaceful stream, the earth and its creatures—made him grunt. Sometimes, even after all these years, it was difficult to reconcile the man known as Buck Colter with what he was inside. Not that the Quakers hadn't done a good job. They had taken a confused little halfbreed and made him more white than Indian. On the outside, at least. But on the inside, where his shadow soul lived, some part of him had rebelled at their dogged preaching about the One God and the white man's road.

Perhaps it was the nature of their god which had confounded him. According to the Quakers, the all-powerful Jehovah was both benevolent and vindictive. A God of whims and moods, whose disposition seemed as vagrant as the winds. If the Good Book was to be believed, he was a God who brought pestilence and famine, flood and death nearly as often as he brought peace and full bellies and the joy of life.

Curiously, the whites even had some notion that this unpredictable god controlled their destiny. Not just as individuals, but as a race. "From the cradle to the grave" was how the Quakers had termed it. Jehovah somehow guided them on a predestined path, making his will known in ways so mysterious that not even the white holy men could fully explain it. Faith, they counseled. A man must have faith and unwavering belief. Yet, depending on his mood of the moment, Jehovah punished the whites almost as often as he blessed them.

Then there was the matter of heaven and hell. That had been a real skullduster. Somewhere, presumably down in the earth's bowels, there was a chamber of fire and brimstone reserved for those who had offended their God. Some burned in everlasting hell, and others floated throughout eternity on a soft feathery cloud. Again according to Jehovah's whimsy, at some murky point in time called the Day of Judgment.

It was simply too much. That a god could tug and pull at a man's life, jerking him around like a doll on a string, was bad enough. But that this same god could slowly roast a man over a pit of fire after his death was the ultimate indignity.

What the Cheyenne believed was perhaps as mystical and fuzzy in its own way, but nonetheless it gave a man an even break in the hereafter. When his shadow soul crossed over to the other side, there was no judgment one way or the other by the spirit beings, and he knew exactly what awaited him in the land beyond. It was a place of cool waters and green grass, fleet ponies and immense buffalo herds. A land without hunger or cold or suffering, where the stewpots were ever full and all men, of whatever tribe, were brothers at last. To get there a man had only to die, whether in battle or of old age, and there were none to bar his path with threats of eternal damnation in a fiery hell.

Still, as a boy and later as a young man, he had seen many similarities between the white man's Jehovah and the red man's spirit beings. The True People believed that their spirit beings must be courted constantly, with offerings and purification rites and visions which would reveal the will of those above. This was further complicated by the fact that the red man had not one god but many, some more powerful than others. Not unlike Jehovah, the spirit beings were at times a capricious lot. When offended they withheld their blessing, turning a man's good medicine to bad, and, more often than not, the reason was left shrouded in mystery. Yet the spirit beings were fair even in their most whimsical moments. They gave a man ample warning, through signs and visions, that his medicine had turned sour. If he chose to ignore their omens, then he had no one to blame but himself.

The essential difference seemed to be that the spirit beings gave a man better odds than did

Jehovah. There were more of them, which spread the risk a bit, and, all things considered, they were of a more tolerant nature than the One God. Other than that, a man would have been hard put to distinguish one from the other. By whatever name—Jehovah or Taime or the Bear Spirit—they messed around in a man's life like a bunch of spiteful children.

Looking back, he could recall that gods and spirit beings hadn't had all that much influence in the path he chose. Wherever he roamed, by whatever name men called him, he would remain more Cheyenne than white. The Quakers hadn't changed that—despite their stern discipline and fiery lectures—nor would time. Inside he would always be An-zah-ti. Little Raven. Only on the outside would he be the one known as Buck Colter.

His decision to follow the white man's road had been prompted solely by the realities of a changing world. Confined to a reservation, penned up much the same as cattle, was no way for a man to live. Particularly An-zah-ti. Grandson of a Cheyenne Dog Soldier. Last in a line of warriors who owed allegiance to nothing save their birthright as free men. That was the way with the True People. A man was obligated to nothing. Not to tribe or clan or family. From the day he gained manhood, his will was his own, and he was free to choose whatever path suited him best.

Strangely, it had been a locomotive that nudged him over the edge. Standing with a group of Cheyenne, he had watched the first steam engine ever to cross Indian Territory grind to a halt outside Fort Sill. The old warrior next to him had stood very still, rigid as a lodgepole, never taking his eyes off the hissing beast. Only after the train pulled out did the ancient one speak.

"The demon spirits have taken the white man's side."

While to the old warrior it was merely a sullen observation, to the young man named An-zah-ti it dawned as an elemental truth. Whether abandoned by the spirit beings or simply trapped in the path of onrushing progress, the red man's day was finished. Come and gone. Their world, the plains and rivers and mountains, was now ruled by the white man. Those who couldn't accept that fact, and change with it, were doomed to remain beggars, living off government charity, for the rest of their lives.

That night he walked away from the reservation.

Standing back from the cabin, he mopped his face again and chuckled to himself. He had come a long way since then. From an educated half-breed without a nickel of his own to a landowner and cattleman in a world apart. With a flaxen-haired wildcat all primed and willing to share his blankets! Back on the reservation the ancient ones would have thought it a fine joke. Little Raven and his white squaw. He could almost hear them laughing and making the vulgar jests that were so appreciated by the True People.

Still and all, there was truth in humor. Rachel was a fine-looking woman, and she would make him a good wife. Together they would build themselves a ranch, raise a whole passel of snot-nosed kids, and have a whale of a time doing it. Maybe even more important, they'd still be chasing each other around the bedroom when it was all said and done. Different as they were in mood and temperament, they struck all the right sparks in all the right places.

Not that they didn't have their little squabbles. Like him spending Sundays working on the cabin instead of squiring her to church. Rachel was a hard-shelled believer, for all her wicked ways, and it irked her no end that he wouldn't set foot in the Lord's house. Though he had agreed to a church wedding, that was his limit, and she hadn't been able to budge him a step further. Which was exactly the way he meant to keep it. She was easy on the eyes, and chain lightning in bed, but she'd just have to get used to the idea that she was marrying a confirmed heathen. Long ago, even before he skipped the reservation, he'd closed the book on that subject.

God came in all shapes and sizes, true enough. Red and white and candy-striped. Something to suit everybody's tastes. But for him it was good old juicy sin, and the Devil be damned.

Chuckling to himself, he hefted another rock and set it in place on what was slowly taking shape as a chimney. All of a sudden his horse snorted, and drew an answering whinny from somewhere behind him, downstream. He whirled about, ducking as the rock tumbled past, and hit the ground with his Colt out and cocked.

Some thirty yards off, grinning like a possum, Ed Overton reined his horse around a dead-fall and rode toward the cabin.

"Gettin' sorta spooked, ain't you, boy? Or was you just practicin'?"

"Take your pick. Only next time yell out before you come sneakin' up on a man."

Colter climbed to his feet and holstered the pistol. Life among the Cheyenne had blunted his fear of death, for the True People took a fatalistic view of man's short journey on earth. His actions of a moment ago had been sheer reflex, born of nothing save an instant and deadly response to a threat. Still, he saw no reason to educate Overton. Let the old rascal think whatever he wanted. In the end, the wary outlived the reckless, and it was hardly a lesson to be shared.

Overton dismounted and ambled forward, still grinning. "Don't blame you a bit. After yesterday I'd be a mite jumpy myself."

"Wasn't much to it. Fellow went lookin' for a fight and he found it, that's all."

"Yeah, but the Circle C don't take kindly to one of their riders gettin' buzzsawed. More'n likely you ain't heard the last of it."

Colter shrugged, revealing nothing. "I just take 'em as they come. One day at a time."

"Good a way as any, I reckon." The old man's grin broadened slightly. " 'Course, after you hear what I got in mind, you might figure on buildin' yourself a fort instead of a cabin."

"How's that?"

"You recollect that idea I mentioned yesterday?" Colter nodded, and he went on. "Well, there's a feller in town I think you oughta meet. Thought we might ride in together tomorrow and palaver with him a little bit."

"Suits me. Only it'll have to be early. I gotta be back to camp by the time the herds start movin'."

"Mebbe after you meet this feller you won't be goin' back to camp."

"You want to spell that out for me?"

"Nope. Time enough in the mornin', after you've heard him out." Overton let go with a thunderous fart and smiled apologetically. "Them whistleberries'll get you every time. Which reminds me. Old shitface himself cornered me yesterday."

"Covington?"

"Yep. Started hintin' around as to how it'd be plumb foolish for anybody to back your play. Meanin' me, naturally."

"What'd you tell him?"

"Didn't tell him nothin'. Be a waste of breath. Tomorrow he'll get his answer, though. In spades."

"One thing about it, you're good at keepin' secrets."

Overton just laughed and headed for his horse.

"Guess I better mosey on. I'll be lookin' for you at my place about sunup."

Colter turned back to the chimney and again hefted the rock. When he stuck it in place, he grunted, struck by a sudden thought. The closemouthed old devil had let slip more than he suspected.

Like maybe he figured it was his fight after all.

EIGHT

Overton and Colter dismounted in front of the hotel and trooped into the lobby. Arnie Grove, the proprietor, blinked when he saw Colter, and started to say something. Then he thought better of it and merely nodded. Overton waved, amiable and smiling, and led the way down the hall. The younger man trailed along behind him, but he couldn't shake the look on Grove's face. Again the thought flitted through his mind that there was something fishy about this whole deal.

All the way into town he had waited for Overton to give him the lowdown. The old reprobate could talk the molars right out of a man's jawbone, and he hadn't paused for more than a couple of breaths during the entire ride. But he hadn't said anything either. At least, nothing about the purpose of their curious little outing. Instead he had talked about cattle and horses and the weather, without once divulging what awaited them in Benton. Colter figured he had his reasons and didn't press it. Which did nothing to lessen his own apprehension. He felt like a blind man walking into a den of bears. With a stubby, white-thatched little elf merrily leading him along by the nose.

Overton hauled up before the door of the last room on the left and knocked lightly. There was a sound of movement inside, and a moment later the door swung open. The man facing them was dressed in range clothes, his features weather-beaten and seamed, plainly someone who had spent a good many years in the saddle. Stamped all over him was the unmistakable look of a cattleman.

"Been expectin' you, Ed. C'mon in." He stepped aside and motioned them into the room.

Overton jerked a thumb over his shoulder. "Tom Powers, meet Buck Colter. He's the young feller I was tellin' you about yesterday."

Powers stuck out his hand. "Pleased to meet you."

"Likewise." Colter let go after a couple of shakes and stepped into the room.

The door closed behind him, and Powers gestured affably. "Have a seat, gents. Take the load off your feet."

Overton plopped down on the end of the bed and waved Colter to a straight-back chair. Powers crossed the room and perched on the edge of a rickety washstand. Then they all sat there and stared at one another for a while. Neither of the older men seemed particularly anxious to open the conversation, and Colter got the feeling he was sitting in on a horse trade. At last Powers cleared his throat and let his gaze come to rest on Overton.

"You two had a chance to talk things over?"

"Nope. All I did was get him here. You're the one doin' the sellin', so I thought you might as well do the talkin.'"

"Fair enough." Powers's glance flicked over to the younger man. "Guess you've heard what's happenin' in New Mexico Territory?"

"There's been some talk," Colter acknowledged. "Pretty bad drouth, the way I heard it."

"Drouth!" Powers snorted. "Shades of hell'd be more like it."

"That bad, huh?"

"Worse'n that. It was just bad when our grass curled up and died. Now we haven't even got water. The Pecos has gone dry as a bone. Not even a trickle."

Colter exchanged glances with Overton. "Never heard of a river dryin' up to nothin'."

Powers laughed sourly. "Well, if you'd like to have a gander at one, just take a ride over Santa Rosa way."

"Maybe after it rains." Colter smiled. "I'm not partial to sleepin' thirsty."

"Neither are cows." Overton grunted. "Tom, why don't you quit beatin' around the bush and give him the straight goods?"

Powers nodded and gave Colter a hangdog look. "Case you ain't figured it out, I've got a spread on the Pecos. 'Bout twenty miles east of Santa Rosa."

"I sorta suspected you was a cattleman."

"Yeah, couldn't hardly be nothin' else, could

I?" Powers's gaze drifted down over his rumpled clothes and scuffed boots. "Trouble is, a cattleman without water ain't no cattleman at all."

"Wouldn't argue with you there."

Overton shifted impatiently on the bed. "Buck, I been knowin' Tom for twenty years, and dealin' with him is worse'n tradin' with an Injun. He just can't get it spit out. Now, the fact of the matter is, he wrote me about his troubles and I wrote him back and told him to ride on over here. What it boils down to is that he's in a bad way to sell some cows. That or stand around and watch 'em die off like flies. I figured he might get shed of most of 'em right here in Benton."

Colter's pulse picked up a beat. "How many head you tryin' to unload?"

Powers swallowed hard. "All I got. Better'n ten thousand mixed stock. Breeders, steers, and the whole shebang."

A deadened silence fell over the room. For a cattleman to sell his breeder stock it had to be hard times. Still, the way Colter sized up this deal, Overton meant to help himself more than he helped the New Mexican. One man's misery was another man's gain.

"That's a lot of cows," Colter observed. " 'Specially with money being tight the way it is."

Overton couldn't suppress a chuckle. "Son, there's no need to start horse tradin'. He's already backed up in a corner. The only thing left to figure out is how many of them cows we're gonna buy."

"We're gonna buy!" Colter shot him a crooked grin. "Hell, Ed, I'm still workin' for wages. I haven't got the money to start off buyin' myself a herd."

"I know that, goddammit. Knew it before I brought you in here. But me and Tom has worked out a deal where you can't afford to pass it up. Go on, Tom, tell him about it."

"Well, there's nothin' much to it really." Powers seemed to perk up a little now that they were talking hard cash. "Ed's gonna buy two thousand head outright. I'm willin' to sell you a thousand head and take your personal note. With him endorsin' it, of course. We figure you can graze 'em all summer and sell 'em this fall. Naturally, I get my cut off the top, but there oughta be a pile left over for you."

"How much a head are these cows of yours gonna cost me?"

"Twelve fifty on the Pecos. Trailin' them back here is your lookout."

Colter did some lightning calculation and suddenly felt a little dizzy. Steers on the fall market would bring easily twice that amount. Which at the very least left him with a cool ten thousand dollars. Free and clear. Enough to buy breeding stock and really set himself up in business. Yet, good as it sounded, there had to be a hook somewhere.

He gave Overton a keen sidewise scrutiny. "What's in it for you?"

The old man smiled slyly. "Figure it out for yourself."

"You're thinkin' you'd rather see a thousand head this side of Cottonwood Creek than the bunch of scrubs I've got now."

"Tell you the truth, boy, I like the way you operate. You got grit, and that's a handy kind o' neighbor to have."

"What about the Association?"

"The hell with 'em. They'll have a hard time kickin' up a fuss about a man who's runnin' a thousand head. Some of them started with less than that, and half of 'em wearin' the wrong brands, too."

"Yeah, but we know somebody that might get his nose out of joint real good. What if these cows of mine just happened to get stampeded to hell and gone? Where'd you be then?"

"Why, Christ A'mighty, if I thought you was piss-willie enough to let that happen, I wouldn't go into it. Course, if it does, then I'm just out a wad of money."

"Funny, I never took you to be a gamblin' man."

"Holy jumpin' Jesus!" Overton eyed him with mock severity. "Boy, haven't you learned nothin' yet? The cow business ain't a thing in the world but pure gamble. You pays your money and you takes your chances. Only this time I ain't bettin' so much on cows as I am on the feller who's gonna own 'em."

Colter thought it over a second and couldn't see that he had anything to lose. "I'm game if you are. When do we get started?"

"We're done started. I just wanted to hear you say it was a deal."

They rose and, after a brief discussion about time and place, shook hands with Powers. At the door, Overton turned back to Powers with a parting word.

"Tom; don't worry none about sellin' the rest of your herd. I've got some of my crew spreadin' the word right now. By suppertime the vultures'll be swarmin' over you like ripe meat." Then he paused, and his smile faded. "Just work it out so none of 'em shows up at the Pecos before Buck here. I wanna make sure we get the pick of the litter."

"You got my word on it, Ed." Powers managed a sallow grin. "Buck can skim off the cream, and I'll even loan him a dipper."

Overton and Colter entered the lobby just as John Covington came through the door. Arnie Grove quickly disappeared into his cubbyhole behind the desk, and the bristles came up on the back of Colter's neck. Somehow he got the feeling that their meeting with Powers had been about as secret as a turd in a punchbowl.

"Mornin', Colonel." Overton halted, looking as though he hadn't a care in the world. "Y'know, just off-hand I'd say Arnie's slippin'. He should've got word to you long before this."

Covington wasn't amused. "Let's forget Arnie. I would like to know what you and Colter have been discussing with this fellow Powers."

Overton's brushy white eyebrows wrinkled in a bulldog scowl. "Sorta early in the mornin' to be nosin' around in other people's business, ain't it?"

"This is Association business, and as a member you shouldn't have to be told that."

"Well, why didn't you say so? That's different." The old man's words were larded with scorn. "Tell you what, Colonel. You trot on back to the Association and inform 'em that me and Buck just bought ourselves a herd of cows. One for him and one for me. Fact is, if you hurry Powers might even have one left over. Probably sell it to you real cheap, too."

Covington's look was cold and ominous. "You know the rules as well as I do. Hired help aren't allowed to own cattle. If you back Colter in this you'll have the whole Association against you. That's something you should give a lot of thought to."

"Colonel, I'm damned if that don't sound like a threat."

"Take it any way you want. It's a fact of life." Covington's gaze slid past the old man. "Colter, if you've got the sense you were born with, you'll chuck this whole business and get on back to your job."

"Guess I can't hardly do that."

"Why not?"

"Well, since you asked, I was just on my way out to the XL to draw my time. Looks like they'll have to get along without me."

"That would be the biggest mistake of your life."

"Think so?"

"You're a fool if you wait around to find out."

Colter smiled, and a curious calm settled over his face. "Colonel, you've got a bad habit of threatenin' people. Sort of rubs a fellow the wrong way. Now lemme tell you what's a fact of life. You mess with me or anything that's mine and I'll put a leak in your ticker. And that's not a threat, it's a lead-pipe cinch."

Stalking off, Colter headed for the street before the cattleman had time to collect his wits. Overton shambled after him, but as he went through the door the old man chuckled and called back over his shoulder, "Better hurry, Colonel. Powers is sellin' them cows like hotcakes."

Covington ground his teeth in quiet fury and watched them out the door. Then he pulled a case from his coat pocket and carefully selected a thin black cigar. When he lit it little flecks of red and gold glistened in his eyes, and a queer look came over his face.

He was still standing there when the match burned his fingers.

NINE

The herd was strung out in a dusty mile-long column. Colter rode point, setting a course northeast across the flat, sun-baked plains of the Texas Panhandle. Glancing up at the angle of the sun, he estimated another four hours of daylight. Somewhere ahead lay Palo Duro Creek, and with any luck at all they would reach it before dusk. There the herd could be watered and bedded down for the night. Already the longhorns had lost their skin-and-bones look, and another night's graze on the lush shortgrass would tallow them out even more. Three weeks on the trail had been hard on man and horse, but for the cattle it had been little short of a picnic. After the arid wasteland along the Pecos, the grassy wind-swept plains of Texas beckoned them on like a glittering star in a darkened sky.

Colter twisted in the saddle and let his gaze rove out over the herd. Leading them was a brindle steer, who on the first day's march had appointed himself pacesetter for the scraggly column. It was one of the enduring curiosities that cowhands often discussed around a campfire at night. Somehow, on every trail drive a certain steer would assume leadership of the herd. By what strange process he assumed the post was a mystery never solved. He simply moved to the head of the herd and stayed there. The rest of the cows followed in his path, allowing him to set the pace, like chicks tagging along behind a mother hen. Whatever the reason, the brindle steer had been worth his weight in gold since departing the Pecos. He was stringy and longshanked, and he shuffled along at a groundeating clip, which meant extra miles covered each day of the drive.

Farther back, Emmet Hungate rode swing on the near side of the herd. The other swing position, along with flank and drag, was left to Slash O riders. Overton had chosen five of his best hands to come along on the drive, and they had earned their keep right from the outset. They were seasoned veterans, with a hard-won savvy of the longhorn breed, and in no small part it was their doing that the drive had gone smoothly to this point. Whatever hitches might have developed simply hadn't and that in itself spoke eloquently of the men who rode the Slash O brand.

Watching them haze bunch quitters back into the herd, listening to their hooting and whistling and the pop of their lariats, Colter still found it a little hard to believe. Slightly over a month back he had been a thirty-a-month hand trying to slap together a ranch in his spare time. Then, in what seemed the blink of an eye, he owned a thousand cows. Just like that!

Not that there weren't a few strings attached. He owed Tom Powers close to thirteen thousand, and Overton had loaned him a thousand working capital, so he was up to his ears in hock. If the roof caved in—stampede, flood, prairie fire, or any one of a dozen natural disasters that could strike a herd—he'd be the rest of his life digging out. But somehow he found himself unable to dwell on such things. Or give them more than passing thought. He had a herd and he had his chance. To be somebody at last.

And, come hell or high water, he didn't mean to muff it.

The same day he quit the XL he had talked Emmet Hungate into throwing in with him. Which, as it turned out, wasn't all that big a chore. Hungate was like an overgrown kid in many ways, and the likelihood of a stiff fight had been the clincher. That it was the Association opposing them hadn't fazed him in the least. Colter was his partner, had been for three years, and that was that. If they couldn't whip the Association between them, then they'd damn well go down swinging.

Yet Colter saw through the act, and appreciated the gesture all the more. Despite his bluster and cocksure ways, Hungate was no dunce. He knew exactly what they faced, and the odds. Knowing and still coming along elevated him to a pretty high perch in Colter's eyes. They had always worked well as a team, and having Hungate at his side brought a measure of comfort about what lay ahead.

Along with the Slash O hands, and a remuda of some thirty horses, they had made it to the Pecos in less than a week. There Colter had spent a couple of days looking over Powers's scattered herds, and before the week was out his crew had gathered three thousand head and driven them to a holding ground. The cream of the crop was none too impressive, though. Colter and his men agreed that the steers were the mangiest-looking excuse for cattle they had ever seen, slat-ribbed, half starved, and glazy-eyed from lack of water. They spent their days standing spraddle-legged, heads bowed, bawling pitifully for something the parched land could no longer give them.

Trail breaking them proved no problem whatever. The normally wild and fiercely defiant longhorns were docile as tabby cats, starved into submission by a year-long drouth. They didn't move fast, for their legs were none too steady, but it took little chousing from the men to start them walking each morning. The third day out brought the herd to the Canadian, which was still flowing, although far below its usual level. Turning their noses to the wind, the cattle scented it a mile off and stampeded toward the river in a towering plume of dust. Colter and the hands thundered along after them, laughing and shouting, almost as delirious as the steers themselves.

Water worked a transformation that was closely akin to magic. The cows swilled and gulped and swelled their bellies, and in the process became longhorns once more. Strengthened, revitalized by the life-giving stream, some of their spirit returned. When the crew started them out next morning it was as if somebody had swapped herds overnight. The steers moved briskly, but with a proud stubbornness, their old cantankerous selves again. Though hardly docile any longer, it was as if they had taken a vote and agreed to tolerate these men who had led them to water. Some bovine instinct convinced them that these puny men on their frisky horses knew the secret—where the rivers flowed. They trudged along behind the brindle steer like trained dogs.

Over the next fortnight Colter allowed the herd to graze its way slowly eastward along the Canadian. The grass, in its own way, worked wonders of a different sort. The steers fleshed out, adding meat and tallow to their skinny rumps. A glossy sheen replaced the mangy look of their coats, and with each passing day they came a step closer to their prime. By the time the herd skirted Tascosa and swung north, they were bright-eyed and bushy-tailed. Longhorns any man could be proud to claim as his own.

The crew was justifiably flush with their success. Granted, something over a hundred weaklings had died along the way, but those that remained were strong and healthy and full of fight. The day they rode out from the Pecos not a man among them thought it could be done—Colter included. The scabby creatures they hazed onto the trail were the next thing to walking death itself. But they had done it. Cursing and whipping and shouting themselves hoarse. With sheer cussedness, they had willed these steers to live.

The wonder of it was not that it had worked, but that it had worked beyond their zaniest expectations. The cattle they herded now bore only scant resemblance to those they had started out with, and in a queer sort of way the men understood how God must have felt at the Creation. Proud as punch and tickled shitless.

Gazing back over the herd now, Colter felt a warm glow of satisfaction down deep in his gut. In another week—ten days at the outside—a thousand of these steers would be grazing on his own range. The Broken Arrow C. A brand he had designed himself with a stub pencil and a scrap piece of paper. One that was somehow fitting, properly symbolic of what had gone before and what remained to come. The joining of past and present. An-zah-ti and the man named Colter.

That evening, shortly before dusk, they circled the herd on a grassy prairie east of Palo Duro Creek. Accustomed now to this nightly ritual, the steers separated into small bunches and started grazing toward the stream. They would feed and water and feed again before bedding down. Along about midnight they would rise, scrambling to their feet in a clatter of hooves and horns, and mill about uncertainly for a few minutes. Why or to what purpose was another of those enduring riddles among men who herded cows. Some dormant instinct, perhaps, to take their bearings and assure themselves that all was well. For after a brief flurry of bawling and nosing the wind, they again sprawled to earth, and stayed there until first light. Then they grazed and watered once more, dotting the plains with steamy mounds of grass-scented dung.

The men made camp upstream from where the cows watered. There was nothing elaborate about the sleeping accommodations or the food. They were traveling light, without chuck wagon or cook, and the comforts commonplace to a trail drive were not part of the bargain. Bed consisted of a couple of sweaty, foul-smelling blankets and a saddle for a pillow. Supper was fast, simple, and filling, if not particularly scrumptious. Thick slabs of salt meat were fried over an open fire while a coffeepot brewed a concoction only slightly less corrosive than anthrax juice. Cornmeal and water were flattened into patties and simmered in the meat grease to make panbread. The whole process could be accomplished in a matter of minutes, and while the best part of the meal was the cigarette that followed, the men wolfed the food down like starved dogs. Sixteen hours in the saddle dulled a man's taste buds and gave him an appetite to make any mother proud.

Leaning back against his saddle, Emmet Hungate let fly with a gassy belch and smiled crookedly. "Boys, I'm here to tell you, there ain't never been grub to equal what the Colter outfit eats. 'Cept one time a joker slipped me some fried pig turds. Now that I think back on it, though, it might've been better'n this after all."

One of the Slash O hands grunted and looked around the fire at the others. "Puts me in mind of a feller I knowed once. There weren't nothin' he wouldn't eat. Hog slop. Grass. Even cow chips if he was up against it. See, the secret was, he never rightly got the taste of it. Larruped it down so fast you could've fed him stewed prickly pear and he'd never knowed the difference."

Hungate reared back in mock indigation. "You sayin' I ain't got no table manners?"

"Nope. Never said that at all. 'Course, up beside you a full-growed grizzly b'ar would look like one of them English dudes in a starchy bib."

That raised a few chuckles, and Hungate went along with a whooping belly laugh. This nightly banter was also something of a ritual, the time when the men unwound and tried to forget their sore backsides. Watching them, Colter took out the makings and started building himself a smoke. While he wasn't as carefree as most cowhands, he enjoyed the sport, and looked forward to it each evening. It wasn't as witty or cutting as the jests employed by the True People, but that in no way lessened his pleasure. As with most things, white men lost the savor of their humor through a temptation to exaggerate the obvious and overlook the unseen.

"Buck, what're you over there dreamin' about?" Hungate was still in a playful mood. "Or maybe it's a little too spicy for this bunch of deacons we got ourselves saddled with."

"Well, I don't reckon it'd singe anybody's ears." He flicked a match and fired up his cigarette. "I was just thinkin' it's gonna be damned sweet to get on home ground again. After the Pecos, Cottonwood Creek is lookin' better all the time."

"Hell, you won't get no argument there." The big man bit off a chunk of Red Devil and commenced working it over. " 'Course, you might change your tune once we get there. Certain parties is liable to have a reception committee waitin' for us. And the greetin' they got in store ain't likely to be what you'd call friendly."

"Last I heard, they climb into their boots one at a time same as we do. Besides, a man gets sort of leery about startin' a scrap if he thinks he's gonna walk away with his balls in his hand."

Hungate peered at him like a nearsighted gorilla. "How's that again?"

"Why, Em, there's all kinds of ways to geld a man." Colter took a drag on his smoke and smiled. "Some of 'em don't even take a knife."

The Slash O riders exchanged puzzled glances, and a wordless accord passed among them. This Colter was a strange duck. The more they got to know him, the less they understood him. Which had a way of giving a man the willies. Particularly when it left him guessing all the time.

After a while the chatter slacked off and the men began hunting their blankets. It had been a long day—sunup to sundown—and they would be at it again with first light. Yet, tired as they were, few of them dropped off to sleep right away. Twisting and turning, they silently considered how somebody went about gelding a man without a knife.

That was one for the books. A real stemwinder.

TEN

Rachel Goddard reined to a halt on the knoll overlooking Cottonwood Creek. Below she spotted four men squatted in the shade of a long building which had been erected downstream from the house. The merest trace of a smile touched her mouth, and she nodded, satisfied that she had timed her arrival perfectly. Clearly they had just finished the noon meal and after a smoke would go back to whatever it was they did with cattle. Which meant that she could get Buck off to herself for a little chat.

One that was long overdue. Far too long.

Unlike many women who acted kittenish and shallow-minded, Rachel could separate charade from reality. Often she felt like an actress on a stage, reciting lines so sweet and simpering that they left a cloying taste in her mouth. But she never lost sight of the fact that it was merely a performance. One born of necessity.

While it grated on her, she had long since come to grips with an elemental truth: The frontier was a man's world. Unfortunate, but nonetheless a fact. And it was the nature of the beast that he liked his women pretty but dumb. The surest way to spinsterhood was to be well read, witty, and intelligent. Men were stiff-necked with pride—far more vain than women—and suspicious of any female capable of rational thought. In some childlike way, they were filled with the need to swagger and bluster and believe themselves superior to anyone that wore skirts.

Which made it ridiculously simple for a smart woman. To get her man she had only to perform on demand. Act out the role of a flighty, simpering, witless little creature, whose virtue was no match for his manly charms. Wedding bells were certain to follow.

Unless things went haywire.

Somewhat reluctantly, she nudged her horse in the ribs and started down the slope. The Goddards' one saddle horse was a clumsy brute, with the gait of a crippled elephant. Her backsides were chafed and tender from the ride over, and every plodding hoofbeat was a small torture in itself. Worse yet, she had never quite gotten the hang of a sidesaddle, and it was only with supreme effort that she managed to hold her seat. All the same, riding astride a horse was considered unladylike, and this was one day she couldn't afford a loss of dignity. Mustering a wide smile, she lifted her chin another notch and rode into the yard.

Colter scrambled to his feet and came forward to meet her. Somehow he appeared embarrassed and pleased all at the same time, and it occurred to her that the element of surprise might well be used to advantage.

"You ought to give a fellow some warnin'." Smiling, he clasped her under the arms and swung her to the ground. "Way I smell, you'll think I've been out wrestlin' bears."

She gave him a dainty peck on the cheek and laughed. "Sugar, there's nothing wrong with good honest sweat. Why, land's sake, sometimes my daddy smells like a hog when he gets through in the fields."

"Yeah, there's worse things, I guess." He faltered a moment and gave her a funny look. Out of the corner of his eye he saw the other men watching intently, and he suddenly felt like a freak in a sideshow. "Something wrong? I mean, why'd you ride all the way over here in this heat?"

"Of course not, silly. Everything's fine. I just wanted to see you, that's all. And see how the ranch is doing."

"Oh."

Colter all of a sudden found himself at a loss for words. The last two weeks had been hectic, and he hadn't had much time for Rachel. In her own sly way she had just said as much, and he felt acutely awkward under her steady gaze.

"Say, I'm not mindin' my manners. C'mon over and meet the boys. Then I'll show you around the place. Done a lot of work since the last time you saw it."

The men climbed to their feet as Colter led Rachel toward them. They were a grungy-looking lot, and reeked of horse sweat, cow manure, and hard work. None of them had had a bath since the last time it rained, and they were just the least bit flustered in the presence of a woman. Particularly one who smelled as if she had just stepped out of a vat of rosewater.

Colter was no less distracted himself, but he gamely started the introductions. "You remember Emmet Hungate, don't you?"

"Why, of course I do." Rachel dimpled up with a bright smile. "Emmet, I swear, seems like you get bigger every time I see you."

"Howdy, Rachel." Hungate flushed and pulled off his hat. "You're lookin' mighty pert yourself."

"And this here's Shorty Thompson."

Thompson, a sawed-off runt with rabbity buck teeth, went red as ox blood. "Ma'am."

"And this long drink of water is Spade Johnson."

Johnson was black as tar pitch, and a full head taller than Hungate. He doffed his battered hat and gave her what passed for a bow. "Proud to make yore acquaintance, ma'am."

"I do declare." Rachel's eyes flashed that funny color of blue, and she looked from one to another with a devastating smile. "Aren't we the lucky ones, though. All you big strong men out herding our cows. Gracious me, I believe I'll sleep easier just knowing Buck has such a fine bunch of men working for him."

The hands swelled up like a flock of peacocks, grinning from ear to ear. Even Shorty Thompson grew a couple of feet under her dazzling smile, and, curiously enough, Spade Johnson broke out in something that had all the earmarks of a dusky blush. Between them they couldn't work up a good spit, so they just stood there, tongue-tied and lightheaded. Thoroughly smitten.

Colter was more embarrassed than before. Grown men standing around making calf eyes and shuffling their feet just because a good-looking woman smiled at them. It was down-right ridiculous, and something that would need watching when Rachel moved into the main house permanent. Otherwise he'd never get any work out of them.

"Boys, tell you what. Why don't you head on out and get the brandin' started again?" He darted a quick glance at Rachel and cleared his throat. "I'll—uh—catch up with you soon as we've had a look around the place."

The men seemed almost relieved to be off the hook. They bobbed their heads, muttering polite good-byes to Rachel, and trooped off toward the corral. Hungate especially couldn't seem to get his eyes uncrossed, and it occurred to Colter that maybe he had been working the big man too hard. All of them, for that matter. Horny cow-hands weren't hardly fit for nothing, and their bumbling performance just now made that plain as a diamond in a goat's ass. Come Saturday night he'd have to send them into Beaver City for a little pole greasing at Madam Lulu's riding academy. Presently the men rode out of the cor-ral, mounted on fresh ponies and looking as though they had just been kissed by the Holy Ghost. Rachel's hex was still working its spell, and they tipped their hats as they passed by, grinning like a trio of stuffed bears.

After they disappeared over the knoll, Colter relaxed a bit and put his arm around Rachel's shoulders. "Long as you're here, I might as well give you the six-bit tour. 'Course, it's still pretty rough, you understand."

"Mercy sakes, honey, you just stop making excuses." She rubbed up against him, all soft and cuddly. "Everybody's got to start somewhere."

"Well, you'll have to admit this isn't no great shakes." He jerked his thumb at the bunkhouse. It was a ramshackle affair that had been slapped together with unbarked logs and chinked with mud fresh from the creek bank. There was every likelihood that in a high wind it would topple over like a pile of matchsticks. "Thing is, we had to have a place to sleep, and I couldn't see lettin' that bunch bed down in our house. It'll do till we get the brandin' done, and then I'll start the boys workin' on something a little more sightly."

Rachel peered through the door and wrinkled her nose, drawing back. It smelled like a wolf den, and all of a sudden she had no wish to see the inside. Colter caught the reaction and quickly steered her toward the main house. As they walked, he pointed out the pole corral and went into a rambling explanation about the crew and their work with the herd.

Upon returning from the Pecos Overton had agreed to let him have two hands full time, and the old man's generosity proved a stroke of luck for the Broken Arrow C. Colter quickly discovered that, with the exception of Emmet Hungate, there wasn't a cowhand in the strip willing to sign on with his outfit. The Association had put out the word, something on the order of a gentle hint that it would be unwise to take sides. It was their opening move, designed to hamstring Colter before he got started, and Overton's help had come just in the nick of time. Even at that, it would be rough sledding right through the fall. Good as they were, Hungate, Johnson, and Thompson were only human. And there were only so many hours in a day. Luckily, the four of them, working dawn to dusk, could manage it. A thousand cows really called for more riders and closer attention, but under the circumstances they'd just have to make do.

"One way or another," he concluded grimly, "we'll pull it off. Them cows are our ticket to lots bigger things."

Rachel was listening with only half an ear. Cows bored her silly, despite the money involved, and just at the moment her mind was wrestling with more earthy matters. Inside the house she examined Colter's handiwork in detail—noting the fine stone fireplace and the planed walls and the spacious kitchen—taking care to display just the right touch of excitement and pleasure. But as they stood in the kitchen, she let her smile slowly dissolve into a girlish pout. It accented both her youth and her oval features, and it was an expression she employed with skill.

"Buck, honey, you haven't forgotten, have you? About the pump? You promised me we'd have one of those fancy inside pumps."

" 'Course I haven't forgotten." He gestured airily toward the corner of the room. "She's gonna be settin' right over there. You can bank on it."

"When?"

"When what?"

"Silly. When are you going to put the pump in?"

"Why, I don't rightly know." He looked about the cabin with a vague uneasiness. "Gotta get the floors laid and rubbed. Cabinets still to be built. Lots of work before this place'll be ready."

"But your daffy old cows come first?"

"You mean before the house gets finished? Hell, yes, they come first. Without them cows we wouldn't even have a johnny pot to stick under the bed. Truth is, we wouldn't even have a bed."

"So everything has to wait for your cows?"

He eyed her suspiciously. "Everything meanin' what?"

"Everything meaning"—Rachel's lip trembled just at the right moment—"our getting married."

"Rachel, for Chrissakes, you're not gonna start that again, are you? We talked it out till I was blue in the face, and I told you we'd get hitched the day I can look after you proper."

"When?"

"When them damn cows are sold, that's when! You got any idea what that'll mean? Ten, maybe twelve thousand dollars, free and clear. We'll be set for life, and you can have your pump and one of them stoves with a big oven and anything else you want. Now, don't you think that's worth waitin' for? Just a little bit longer."

Rachel walked to the window and stood looking out at the creek. After a long while she turned, and a single tear dribbled down over her cheek. "What if I told you I was in a family way?"

Colter blanched, and it was a moment before he found his voice. "Are you?"

Perhaps more than most, Rachel had realized early in life that women were blackmailers by instinct. It came natural to them, soon after their breasts ripened and their hips filled out; in negotiating emotional business with a man, their bodies were both the bait and the hook. But, having dangled the bait and set the hook, she now found herself unable to land the prize.

"No, I'm not." She shook her head, and something devilish flickered in her eyes. "Matter of fact, I got a visitor last night. So if you've got any sneaky ideas, you can just forget them. At least for the next few days, anyhow."

"Goddamn, you're a crafty little vixen, aren't you?"

Colter crossed the room and took her in his arms. Her gaze lifted, beguiling and yet somehow guileless, and her lips parted. He kissed her long and hard, cupping her breast in his hand, and she moaned softly. At last, when he released her, a grin covered his face.

"Come first frost, you and me are gonna start makin' babies. And that's a promise you can bank on."

She gave him a slow wink and smiled wickedly. "Like you said, lover—one way or another."

ELEVEN

Independence Day had come and gone, and the land sweltered beneath a gauzy summer sky. High overhead the sun hammered down with brute force, and small clouds scudded across the far horizon like puffs of smoke. It was a day when cows sought refuge along shady creek banks and men stirred about reluctantly, if at all. The slightest effort left a man soaked in sweat, and the broiling heat sapped his energy like a wolfberry sucked dry of its juices.

Standing in the door of his mercantile, Luther Emerson mopped his face and idly wondered if the heat spell would ever end. Not even a vagrant wind offered relief, and the steamy air was suffocating in its very stillness. Like the inside of a Dutch oven on a slow fire. Emerson grunted with disgust and let his gaze wander slowly along the street. What he saw did little to improve his mood: one horse hitched outside the Yellow Snake Saloon and a wheezy old dog flopped in the shade of the hotel porch. He scowled and let go a sour belch.

Big day in Benton. The kind that gives a merchant the stomach flutters. Or worse.

Looking west, he saw two specks appear on the river trail, blurred and distorted by the shimmering haze. Slowly they took shape, and after a while he could separate horse from rider. With nothing better to do, he waited and watched, curiosity whetted by the mere sight of another human being. Only in this case there were two of them. And out on a day not fit for man or beast. Then the riders passed the schoolhouse, and he could make them out at last.

Overton and Colter.

Another sour burp rumbled up from his gut, and for a moment he considered retreating into the store. Then he decided the hell with it and stood his ground. He'd known both these men since he came to the Strip, and nobody was going to make him turn his back on friends. Emerson waved as they rode past, and the cattlemen nodded, sober as a couple of judges. Their eyes lingered on him only a moment and swept away in a careful scrutiny of the horse and the dog and the empty street.

The merchant considered himself something of a philosopher, a student of human nature, but he nonetheless found Overton and Colter an unlikely pair. Over the last month he had speculated on it at length, and he still hadn't arrived at a satisfactory answer. Yet, whatever it was that bound them together, it had been sorely put to the test.

Association members had visited every merchant in Benton, and their roundabout hints amounted to little more than veiled threats. Anyone who extended further credit to Overton or Colter might find his regular customers trading elsewhere. It was an economic squeeze which merited consideration, and the storekeeper who ignored the warning could well find the wolf standing at his door.

Still, a more ominous note had only recently been sounded. John Covington had disappeared in late June, and upon his return the *Benton Banner* devoted half its front page to his trip. Representatives of every Cattlemen's Association in the West had met in Denver and formed the International Range Association. The bluntly stated purpose of this new organization was to eliminate rustlers, discourage sodbusters, and block shoestring outfits from expanding their holdings. That the large spreads were in dead earnest had already become apparent. Several small ranchers in Wyoming, accused of rustling, had either been run out of the country or killed.

Like ripples in a pond, the effects of the Denver meeting had also been felt in No Man's Land. Within the past week the rules of the game had changed. Before, cows from the Slash O or the Broken Arrow C that strayed across their boundaries were simply choused back onto homeground. Now they were shot in their tracks and left to rot in the boiling plains sun.

Overton and Colter were caught in a nutcracker, and slowly being scrunched.

Emerson watched them dismount in front of the Yellow Snake and push through the batwing doors. It bothered him that such things could happen, particularly to honest men simply trying to make their mark. But then, business was business, and a merchant was merely a seller of goods. However sympathetic, Luther Emerson was not his brother's keeper. He belched, rubbing his stomach, and retreated into the store.

Overton and Colter stopped just inside the doorway, letting the dank, musty smell of whiskey and stale tobacco bathe them in its coolness. After a moment the old man's eyes adjusted to the dim interior, and he headed toward the back of the saloon. There, seated at a rear table, was a solitary drinker. The only customer in the place.

Colter was only a step behind as they halted before the table. The stranger looked up, and Overton smiled. "Howdy. Your name Williams, by any chance?"

"Only when I'm sober." The man smiled back and gestured with his glass. "Drag up a chair and join me."

Overton eased himself into a chair opposite the man, and Colter took a seat on the far side of the table, next to the wall. Craning around, Overton signaled the bartender and then turned back. "Understand you're buyin' cows for the government."

"That's my business," Williams acknowledged. "Why, you got some cows you wanna sell?"

"Mebbe. All depends on the deal." Overton jerked his head at the younger man. "Me and my friend here ain't never dealt with the government, but we've got plenty of cows."

"Glad to hear it. I've been sittin' here all day and there's only one feller dropped by. And I couldn't rightly say he came lookin' to sell."

Overton exchanged glances with Colter and sank back in his chair. "Wouldn't have been a gent by the name of Covington, would it?"

"Yep, that's the one. Colonel John Covington. Made a point out of tellin' me he used to be a colonel in the militia."

"What else did he tell you?"

"Nothin' worth listenin' to, just exactly." Williams paused and took a swig of his drink. " 'Ceptin' I'd be buyin' myself a peck of trouble if I did any tradin' with a couple of fellers named Colter and Overton."

"Sneaky bastard." Overton's jowls tightened, and he sort of grunted to himself. "Just in case you're wonderin', that soberpuss sittin' next to you is Colter, and I'm Overton."

Williams smiled. "Figured you was when you come through the door. Way I got the story, you two were about the only ones that'd be willin' to talk to a contract buyer."

"That a fact? What'd Covington say?"

The barkeep appeared with a fresh bottle and two glasses and placed them on the table. Williams waited until he was out of earshot, then went on as Overton poured a round of drinks.

"He didn't mince any words, I can tell you that. Said the Association hereabouts wasn't interested in sellin' to the government, and that meant everybody but you fellers. Then he let it drop that I'd be borrowin' trouble if I tried dealin' with you."

"Don't s'pose he made that any plainer?"

"Nope. I asked what he meant, and he said a word to the wise was sufficient. Gave it to me real short and frostylike, then he just turned around and waltzed out."

"That's his way, awright. Frosty as a witch's tit."

Colter pulled out the makings and sprinkled tobacco onto curled brown paper. "You say he told you the Association wouldn't deal with the government. Why is that?"

"Same reason lots of folks won't," Williams observed. "The government don't pay market price."

"How come?"

"Mostly 'cause they're buyin' the beef for Injuns. The Bureau figures nobody's gonna sell us choice stuff anyway, so they make us contract at a set price for future delivery."

"Delivered where?"

"Rosebud reservation, up in Dakota Territory." Williams studied him a moment, noting the high cheekbones and gray eyes, and started to say something. Then a flicker of doubt touched his face, and he set the thought aside. "Up there we got mostly Sioux and Cheyenne."

"How much you payin' for cows?"

"Twenty-four a head. Flat rate. How you get 'em there is your business. 'Course, a train's the easiest way. We got holdin' pens down in Valentine. That's across the line in Nebraska."

Colter looked around at Overton. "Sounds sort of skimpy to me. Buyers up in Dodge are payin' five, six dollars more a head."

"That's what they're payin' today," Overton corrected him. "Come fall the bottom's liable to drop out and they'll be payin' a damn sight less."

"You've got a point there." Williams smiled and refilled their glasses. "We're lookin' for delivery in late September. Contract now and you've got yourself a guaranteed price."

"Yeah, but we're standin' the freight." Colter pursed his lips and frowned. "Looks to me like we'd come up with a short payoff."

"Now hold your horses." Overton leaned forward, fixing him with a bright stare. "We're fightin' two fights. The Association and a cow market that sometimes goes dipsy-doodle in the fall. You just think about it for a minute."

"You already had your mind made up before we rode in here, didn't you?"

"Not just exactly. But I'm for it now that we've heard the price. Y'know, there's times it pays to hedge your bet."

Colter glanced at his cigarette, all but forgotten in the conversation. After striking a match, he lit it and took a couple of puffs, then looked up. "Well, you've been right so far. Guess I might as well tag along for the ride."

Williams brightened and came erect in his chair. "Gents, I think you made a wise decision. Come fall, twenty-four might look damned good."

The doors slammed open, and Wash Sealy walked into the saloon. Glancing toward the back, he spotted the three men and made his way to the rear of the bar. He waited for a drink, downed it, and then turned. Hooking his elbows over the bar, he glowered across the room at Williams.

"Mister, you don't listen so good. The Colonel gets sorta peeved when folks cross him up. Savvy what I mean?"

Colter came out of his chair and moved around the table. "Sealy, you're buttin' in on private business. Suppose you trot on back to Covington and tell him it didn't work."

Sealy nailed him with a baleful frown. "Better back off, kid. You mess with me and you'll get beefed. 'Case you ain't heard, I play dirty pool."

The bartender reached under the counter for his shotgun, but the metallic whirr of a gun hammer stopped him cold. He glanced across the room and found himself staring down the barrel of Overton's pistol. The old man's snowy mustache lifted in a grin. "Everybody just stand real still till my friend calls the tune."

Colter advanced on the Circle C foreman. "You shook the wrong tree. Time to put your money where your mouth is."

Sealy was no slouch in a rough-and-tumble fight. A ramrod held his job, in no small part, by the sheer fact that he could whip the rest of the crew. He was built on the stocky side, corded with muscle, and had arms like gnarled oak trunks. Time and experience, and countless barroom brawls, had taught him one lesson: The man who makes the first move generally walks away unscarred. And now he made that move.

Feinting with a left, he shifted and uncorked a whistling right. The blow caught Colter flush on the jaw, and he went down like a sack of mud. As he hit the floor he rolled, dazed but unhurt, and a heavy boot landed where his head had been. Sealy launched another kick, but Colter saw this one coming. Arching his back, he caught the foreman's leg in midair, scissored it between his own legs, and yanked hard. Sealy fought to hold his balance but lost, and as he fell Colter rolled clear and scrambled to his feet. Stung by the sucker punch, and the strength of the man behind it, Colter wasted no time. Twisting sideways, he struck out with a short, chopping kick. The blow caught Sealy smack on the button as he came off the floor. His nose flattened into a bright red blossom, and he hurtled backward, bowling over a spittoon as he skidded to a halt upside the bar. Covered with blood and tobacco spit and sodden cigar butts, he lay absolutely still, out cold.

Colter grabbed Sealy's shirt collar and began dragging him toward the door. Glancing back, he gave Overton a tight grin. "Go ahead with our deal. I'm just gonna dump this load of shit out in the street, where he belongs."

Overton nodded and turned back to the table, holstering his pistol. Williams had a strange look in his eye, and as Colter went through the door his gaze shifted to the old man.

"That partner of yours has a funny way of fightin'."

"Yeah? How's that?"

"Well, I don't know just exactly. Sort of puts me in mind of the way them reservation Injuns scrap with one another. Lots of kickin' and fancy wrestlin'. Don't hardly never use their fists, though. That's what I was gettin' at."

Overton stared at him a moment, mulling it over. It was an interesting thought, one that he had considered and discarded a few years back when he first saw Colter. Setting it aside for the moment, he laughed and began filling the glasses.

"Hell, a feller could've picked up them tricks in lots of places. Only thing that counts is that it works."

Williams's gaze shifted as Colter came through the door, brushing off his shirt. All of a sudden the subject ceased to interest him. "Yeah, I guess you're right. How many cows was it you fellers wanted to sell, anyway?"

TWELVE

Colter skirted the herd shortly before noon and rode toward camp. Slash O riders were stationed at the cardinal points, containing the cows on the holding ground and hazing bunch quitters back into the fold. Various ranches, mostly those south of the Beaver, had sent reps to inspect the cows as they were gathered and brought into roundup. Some of the reps nodded as he rode past, but most simply looked through him as if he didn't exist. Which didn't bother him one way or another. Their wages were being paid by men who hated his guts, and that tended to shade a cowhand's thoughts. He understood and held no grudges, for, when it was all said and done, he just didn't give a good goddamn.

One more week. That's all he needed. Then he'd rub their noses in it and do a little crowing of his own.

Just the thought of it brought a smile to his face, and, approaching camp, he kneed the sorrel gelding into a prancing trot. The Slash O chuck wagon was off beside a grove of cottonwoods near Clear Creek. Overton was standing upwind of the fire, swigging a cup of coffee and, from the looks of things, badgering the cook. It was the old man's favorite sport, next to rattling off bowel-rending farts, and he took devilish glee in making a pest of himself. Turning, his sour look widened into a grin as Colter reined to a halt and swung down from the saddle.

"By God, Buck, you got here just in time. I was tellin' Slick this coffee's bitter as bear piss, and he keeps sayin' my taster's out of whack. C'mon and get yourself a cup and settle the argument."

"Humph!" Slick grouched something under his breath and slammed the lid on a pot. "You keep at me and bear piss is what you're likely to wind up drinkin'."

The cook was an old horse wrangler who had taken a bad spill some years back and come out with a game leg. Overton had nicknamed him Ol' Slick and Greasy, a commentary of sorts on his cooking, and over a period of time it had been shortened to merely Slick. Colter suspected that both men enjoyed this running battle of wits and would probably be lost without each other to pick on.

Watching them now, he smiled and shook his head. "You're not gettin' me betwixt and between. I'll pass, and you two can hash it out amongst yourselves."

"Aw, it don't make no never mind," Overton rasped. "Whatever he calls this sheep dip, it still ain't fit for human consumption."

"Balls o' fire!" Slick cackled. "You talk like it

was natural-born people drinkin' it. This outfit don't hire nothin' but peckerheads and dim-dots."

Slick gimped around the fire, peeking inside a battery of Dutch ovens and shifting blackened skillets over a bed of coals. From the smell of things it was sourdough biscuits, fried steak, and spotted-pup rice for dinner. Overton caught himself just as he was about to lick his lips, and turned away toward the shade of the trees.

"C'mere, Buck. Rest your backsides a spell and tell me what's happenin' on the gather."

Colter hunkered down and started building himself a smoke. "There's nothin' much to tell. Hungate and my boys are workin' Cottonwood Creek, and your crew is still split between here and there. I made a circle this mornin', and from the looks of it, things are slowin' down. The bunches they're flushin' are lots smaller than what we was gettin' a couple of days ago."

Overton grunted and tugged reflectively at his mustache. "What's your tally on the ones we got gathered?"

"You talkin' about Pecos steers or the whole kit and caboodle?"

"Just the Pecos steers."

"Little shy of twenty-six hundred, includin' what I saw the boys drivin' this mornin'."

"That leaves us four hundred short of the contract." Overton hawked and spit, then jerked his chin toward the south. "You figure they're out there?"

"Hard to tell." Colter gazed out over the rolling plains and the herd gathered south of camp.

"We'll have a better idea the next couple of days."

"Damn sure better have," Overton snorted. "We gotta have 'em to railhead in Meade come Monday mornin', and in case you forgot, that's less'n a week off."

"We'll make it. I figure it a four-day drive at the outside."

"Well, if we come up short on Pecos steers I can always throw in some of my stuff to make up the difference." The old man smiled to himself and glanced sideways out of the corner of his eyes. "Guess them heathen redsticks wouldn't mind if we throwed in a batch of good stuff."

Colter shifted uncomfortably and took a long pull on his cigarette. "Most likely not."

Overton glimpsed the reaction, and bit down on the temptation to probe further. "What about them Association reps—they givin' you any trouble?"

"No more'n we expected. Had a few squabbles here and there, but nobody's set off any fireworks yet."

"Damned if that ain't got me buffaloed." Overton rubbed the wiry stubble on his chin and frowned. "Covington ain't the kind to make hollow threats. I keep wonderin' what he's got up his sleeve, and when he's gonna spring it."

"Maybe he's plannin' on havin' the herd stampeded between here and Meade. That way he could blame it on somebody else, and the Association would come out smellin' like a rose."

"Yeah, that's his way of thinkin', right

enough." The old man spat and splattered a horsefly against a tree. "Shifty sonovabitch. I'd like to put his nuts in a vise and ask him a couple of questions. Betcha we'd get some answers then."

"Like as not we'll get the answer sooner'n we want. Way I see it, he's got to make his move pretty quick."

"Mebbe. Mebbe not. There's just no tellin' with a sneaky bastard like that. His kind's slippery as greased owlshit, and the hell of it is, they don't think like we do. Which, in a manner of speakin', gives 'em an edge right from scratch."

Overton's observation, though shrewd and penetrating, was hardly enlightening. Every morning for the past two months both men had expected to awaken and find that some calamity had befallen them overnight. Poisoned waterholes. Cattle stampeded. Or perhaps a hand bushwacked off in some desolate stretch of country. They were at first amazed, and not a little relieved. But with the passing of time they became, in turn, befuddled and finally warily dumbfounded.

Absolutely nothing had happened.

In early September, with preparations underway to gather the contract herd, they fully expected some countermeasure from the Association. Fall roundup in No Man's Land rarely started before the latter part of the month, with the first cold snap. Generally, the Association set a specified date and anyone who jumped the gun did so at his own risk. The cattlemen preferred to gather as a group—for they trusted fellow members only slightly more than they trusted common rustlers—and every outfit wanted to make certain that its own interests were protected.

That Overton and Colter had thumbed their noses at still another established custom was no small matter. They were aware that the move would spark bitter resentment throughout the strip, and took steps to head off trouble before it started. Late in August they informed every outfit along the Beaver of their intent to conduct an early roundup and the reason behind it. In order to fulfill the government contract, the herd had to be shipped from Meade no later than the middle of the month. As a final gesture of good will—and a device to undercut any suspicion of rustling—they requested that each rancher send a rep to oversee the gather. Having done all they could, they sat back and waited. Fully expecting the lid to blow off at any moment.

Again, nothing had happened.

Nor had there been even a hint of trouble during the last week, while the roundup was underway. Though they kept to themselves, reps from every outfit showed up and quietly went about the business of cutting out cows marked with their brands. There had been a few minor disputes, mostly over yearlings that had escaped previous gathers, but nothing that threatened to get out of hand. Queer as it seemed, everybody acted as if they were trying to avoid trouble. Almost as though the reps had been ordered to give the Slash O and the Broken Arrow C all the leeway they wanted.

Mulling it over now, Overton let go with a little pipsqueak of a fart, a sure sign that his innards weren't functioning properly. "Tell you the truth, it's got the livin' bejesus worried out of me. Things are just too goddamned peaceful. To my way of thinkin', that's the worst sign there is."

Colter ground out his cigarette and tried to shift his mind back to the business at hand. Just for a while there his thoughts had wandered off to Rachel, and the dull throb between his legs made it difficult to concentrate. Two lousy weeks since he'd seen her, and him horny as a preacher in a cathouse full of naked women. Somehow, before the drive to Meade, he'd have to pay her a visit. Even if it was short and sweet and mostly *adios*.

Commotion off in the distance jarred him loose from his bittersweet ruminations, and he saw two horsemen riding toward camp. Hungate and Wash Sealy. He couldn't make out what they were saying, but it hardly mattered. Plain to see that they were mad as hell and just on the verge of locking horns. Uncoiling, he climbed to his feet and glanced down at the old man.

"Maybe that trouble you've been expectin' just found us. Sealy wouldn't come nosin' around here unless the Colonel sent him."

Colter made it back to the chuck wagon as Hungate dismounted and stalked toward him. One glance told him that the big man was in a towering rage. Wash Sealy was only a step behind, and looked mad enough to chew nails.

Whatever it was, they had clearly been trading insults all the way into camp.

Hungate let fly with a fiery blast. "Buck, this sorry, connivin', motherless sonovabitch is tryin' to claim one of our cows. Says we used a runnin' iron. Can you believe that? A gawddamned runnin' iron!"

Sealy stomped around in front of the big man and squared off. "Hungate, you call me one more name and by Jesus Christ I'll clean your plow right here. Quicker'n scat."

That seemed to amuse Hungate, and he peered down at the foreman with a mocking smirk. "You little runt, this outfit's already hauled your ashes once. You wanna try for seconds?"

Sealy purpled and swelled up like a bantam cock. His nose was still bent out of shape from the impact of Colter's boot, but that didn't seem to faze him in the least. Snarling something unintelligible, he raised his fists and waded in.

"Hold it!"

Colter's grated command stopped him short and brought a groan from Hungate. The big man slowly lowered a meaty paw that was only a second away from coldcocking the Circle C foreman.

"Sealy, what the hell are you doing here, anyway?" Colter spun him around by the shoulder. "Your outfit's had a rep here since we started, and so far as I know he's got no complaint."

"Keep your hands to yourself, Colter." Sealy edged sideways so that he was facing both men. "There's nothin' that says I can't have a look-see at what's happenin'. And a damn good thing, too. I caught your boys chousin' a Circle C cow that's been worked over just sure as hell."

They studied each other a moment, and Colter's face went stone cold. "Let's just forget that you're lyin' through your teeth. You tell me how a Broken Arrow can be laid down over a Circle and I'll slap your saddle on that cow and let you ride him home."

Hungate snorted. "Hell, he can't, Buck. The whole thing's a crock of shit. The cow he's talkin' about is one of them Pecos steers."

"How about it?" Colter demanded.

Sealy's face mottled with rage. "Your time's comin', Colter. You know that? There's people standin' in line to punch your ticket."

Wheeling about, Sealy stomped back to his horse, swung aboard, and galloped out of camp. They watched after him in silence awhile, and finally a baffled frown crept over Hungate's features.

"Buck, what'n the name of Christ was that all about?"

"I'm not real sure, but I got an idea they were tryin' to dummy up a rustlin' charge against us."

"You nailed it dead center." Overton walked forward and joined them. "If you'd let him have that cow, they'd have run us out of the country."

"Or strung us up," Colter speculated aloud.

The three men exchanged sober glances, and then turned back to watch Sealy pounding west toward the Circle C. After what seemed a long while, the old man grunted and took a swipe at his snowy mustache.

"Chalk one up for our side."

THIRTEEN

The hotel in Meade was considered the fanciest digs in western Kansas. It had cushy beds, a hand-painted porcelain basin in each room, and tubs of scalding water for those willing to pay the tariff. Standing on a corner in the heart of town, it was a two-story structure with a wide, shaded veranda fronting both streets. The rooms were spacious and airy, and the furniture was several notches above what most of the customers had in their own homes. But, for all its plush comforts, the Osgood Hotel's chief claim to fame was its food. Unlike most railhead hotels, it had its own cafe, which the owner insisted on calling a restaurant. This ritzy distinction was lost on the natives, but it in no way lessened their gusto for the Osgood's bill of fare. The cafe served three meals a day, and from morning till night it was a swarming beehive of hearty eaters.

Shortly after the crack of dawn, Overton led Colter and Hungate down the carpeted stairs and into the dining room. Loading down at the cattle pens was scheduled to begin sharply at eight, and the three men were more interested in speed than the quality of the grub. Despite the early hour, a scattering of customers was already being served, and Overton took that as a good sign. Ambling across the room, he selected a table next to a window and gingerly lowered himself into a chair. Colter and Hungate took seats opposite him and tossed their hats on the windowsill.

Overton winced as he adjusted his rump to the chair, and began casting about for a waitress. After signaling a plump, rosy-cheeked girl, who bustled by with a loaded tray, he turned back to the younger men.

"Boys, I'm gettin' too old for this nonsense. My ass is galled so bad it feels like I just sprouted a patch of boils. Had to sleep on my belly the whole goddamned night."

"Hell, Ed, it was only four days." Hungate's expression was just short of a smirk. "Long as you've been forkin' horses, I'd think your butt would've turned to whang leather."

Overton shot him a dour look. "There was a day I could've rode circles around the likes of you. Not too long ago, neither. Trouble is, here lately I've been sittin' in a rocker more'n a saddle. That's what comes of gettin' old and lazy and—"

"Lardassed." Hungate chortled.

"Y'know, sometimes you act like you've got the brain of a pissant and the mouth of a bullfrog. Decent folks are supposed to have sympathy for a man in misery, and goddammit, you're sittin' there lookin' at one right now."

Colter grunted and gave him a wry smile. "Nobody's fault but your own. There wasn't a reason in the world for you to come along. And I told you so before we ever started."

"I had my reasons. Whole bunch of 'em." Overton grimaced as little prickles of fire darted across his rump. " 'Case you forgot, most of them cows is wearin' my brand."

"Same held true when we trailed 'em up from the Pecos. But I don't recollect you pitchin' a fit to play nursemaid then."

"Well, there's one thing about it," Hungate interjected. "Goin' home, you can just lay out in the back of the chuck wagon and rest that sore butt of yours in style."

Overton ignored the remark. "Way you two run a cattle drive, it's a good thing I come along. Back in the old days they wouldn't have let you fetch spit. Much less boss a crew."

"Judas Priest!" Hungate groaned. "Here we go again about the old days. Now you just watch. The very next thing he says is gonna be how the old-timers had it all over us young whippersnappers."

Before Overton could frame an answer, the apple-cheeked waitress marched up to the table and gave them a brisk smile. "Good morning! What can we do for you today?"

Hungate reared back and flicked one eyelid in a lecherous wink. "You really wanna know?"

The girl gave him a swift appraisal and wrinkled her nose. "Ask me the next time you wash behind your ears."

Colter and Overton burst out laughing, and Hungate went red as ox blood. After the girl had taken their orders and brought coffee, they settled down and concentrated on the steamy mugs. It had neither the aroma nor the thick, gritty flavor of Slick's coffee, but it warmed their innards and got everything functioning again.

Overton slurped and discreetly broke wind a couple of times, then sat back with an owlish frown. "Y'know what throws me? I'm sittin' here in a fancy hotel, swiggin' coffee, gettin' waited on hand and foot, and I still can't rightly believe it. Don't you see, it's like wakin' up in one of them spiffy whorehouses and findin' out it wasn't a dream after all."

"You mean the Association?" Colter asked. "Gettin' the herd here?"

"Bet your bottom dollar that's what I mean. It just don't make any sense. They could've chopped our legs out from under us a hundred different ways, but here we sit with the train waitin' and a load of cows all set to go. I don't mind admittin', it's plain got me stumped."

"Mebbe Covington's not as tough as ever'body thinks he is." Hungate's tone belied his words. "I mean, mebbe he just figured he'd wind up losin' more'n he won."

"You're right about him not being all that tough," Colter agreed. "But it's like Ed says. He's slippery as a barrel of eels, and mean clear through. Could be he's got the game rigged some way we haven't tumbled to just yet."

"Well, it beats the shit out of me," Hungate said. "I ain't the brightest feller in the world, but

I'm here to tell you, they passed up some mighty good chances. Christ, they could've stampeded that herd fifty times between here and the Beaver."

"That's exactly what I'm gettin' at," Overton growled. "The thing that's got me bumbuzzled is, why didn't they?"

Colter built himself a smoke and lit it while they sat there mulling it over. Presently he took a long drag and let it out in quick little spurts. "One thing's for damn sure. Until we get a peek at his hole card, we're just wastin' time tryin' to second-guess him."

Hungate squinted quizzically. "Just how the hell would you suggest we go about gettin' a look at his hole card?"

Across the table Overton stiffened and came erect in his chair. "Boys, I don't know much about cards, but the Devil himself just waltzed through the door."

Colter and Hungate twisted around and stared open-mouthed as Covington entered the dining room. With him was a man they had never seen before, dressed in the somber clothes of an undertaker. Covington and the stranger stood in the doorway a moment and then headed for a table at the rear of the cafe. Not once, while they were crossing the room or after they were seated, did they so much as glance at the gaping cattlemen.

At last Hungate let out a gusty snort. "I'll kiss your ass and bark like a fox."

"In spades," Overton rasped.

Colter stared at his cigarette as if he had never

seen one before, and after a while he glanced across the table. "Ed, I don't know about you, but for my money that fisheyed sonovabitch didn't just happen to turn up in Meade, Kansas, on the day we're shippin' a load of steers."

"That ain't the half of it." Overton jerked his head toward the hotel lobby. "Them jaybirds came down from upstairs, which means they spent the night here, and more'n likely Covington hit town before we did."

"Yeah, but what the hell for?" Hungate shot back. "A man don't ride forty miles just to watch the trains come in."

"All depends. Mebbe the Colonel had himself *one particular* train in mind."

"The one we're shippin' on?"

"Emmet, lemme put it to you this way. Long as I've known John Covington, I never heard tell of him comin' to Meade. That give you any clues?"

" 'Course it does. But that still don't answer the question. What's he aimin' to do?"

"Christ, I ain't no swami. My crystal ball got busted a long time ago."

"Wish you'd had it fixed," Colter observed dryly. "How about that other jasper? Ever seen him before?"

The old man looked across the room and after a moment shook his head. "Nope. Can't say as I have. Sort of a queer-lookin' bird, ain't he? Like he'd just come from a buryin'."

"Or was headed to one."

Overton's gaze whipped around. "Buck, do

you get the feelin' that somebody's baited a trap with our name on it?"

"Like you said." Colter nodded. "In spades."

The girl appeared with a tray just then and commenced slamming plates down in front of them. When she walked away, the men hefted their silverware mechanically and began picking at the food.

All of a sudden, their appetites were gone.

The rest of the crew was waiting for them when they reached the stockyards. Colter and Hungate took a little ribbing about staying overnight in a hotel, but it was all in good fun. Their quarters for the next week would be a boxed-off stall in a cattle car, and none of the hands especially envied them the ride. Some dozen or so longhorns would be sharing their accommodations, just on the other side of the partition, and it promised to be a fragrant trip.

Loading chutes were dropped into place, and the men began hazing cows up the ramp and into boxcars. It was a hot and dirty business, mostly shouting and cursing and prodding, worse than the cattle drive itself. The cows either balked at the head of the chute, refusing to budge another foot, or spooked halfway up the ramp and started a stampede in the wrong direction. As the morning wore on the men gradually became grime-streaked and sweaty and thoroughly out of sorts. Most of them were skinned and bleeding from scrambling to safety atop fences, and their curses became a little viler with each new mishap.

But as the sun rose high, nearing the noon hour, the last car was loaded. Colter slammed the doors shut, threw the latch, and jumped to the ground. It had taken two full trains to handle the herd, and he felt immensely relieved to see them safely loaded and ready to pull out. Wiping his face with a filthy bandanna, he walked down the tracks and joined Overton at the south end of the cow pens.

"Guess we're ready to roll." Leaning against the fence, he started rolling the first smoke he'd had in three hours. "Can't say as I'm lookin' forward to the ride, though."

The old man grunted, unusually solemn. "Take a quick peek over my shoulder."

Colter edged away from the fence and looked past him. Standing some distance away, John Covington was delivering a hot lecture to the stranger they had seen earlier. The man was nodding, saying little, wholly absorbed in the flow of words.

"How long they been there?"

"Ever since you and the boys started loadin' the last train. Just stood over there watchin' like a couple of hawks."

Colter suddenly stiffened, and his eyes narrowed in a thin line. The stranger shook hands with Covington, gave him a stony smile, then turned and marched toward the rear of the train. He was carrying a small warbag, and from the bulge in his coat Colter suspected he was packing a hideout gun in a shoulder holster.

"Ed, this deal is gettin' riper all the time. That

undertaker-lookin' gent just climbed aboard the caboose."

Overton turned in time to see the stranger mount the steps and disappear through the door of the caboose. Across the way Covington just stood there, staring at them, like death warmed over. When they finally glanced in his direction, he gave them a gloating smile, almost as if he were about to lick his lips. Then he wheeled about and struck off toward town.

They stared after him for a minute in silence, more confused than ever. At last Overton hawked and spat a wad of phlegm in the dust. "Wish to Christ I knew what the sneaky bastard was up to."

"Ai!" Colter realized only much later that he had answered in Cheyenne.

The train whistle blasted them out of their funk. Colter spun around and saw Hungate motioning to him from a forward car. The old man grabbed his hand, looking sort of unsettled, and pumped hard.

"Watch after yourself, boy. Don't let your guard down for a minute. Y'hear me?"

The boxcars jarred and the train started moving. Colter took off running up the tracks and called back over his shoulder.

"Quit your frettin'. Look for me when you see me."

FOURTEEN

The train pulled into Valentine shortly before noon. After considerable backing and lurching, it was switched to a siding and came to a halt beside the cattle pen. Frank Williams and close to a dozen cowhands were waiting as the engine hissed a final belch of steam and seemed to collapse like a weary dragon. The men clambered down from the fence, glad to have the waiting done with, and began muscling a loading chute into place. Williams walked off down the tracks, checking each car as he headed toward the rear of the train.

Down the line, the roof door slid back on a boxcar and Colter appeared through the opening. He hoisted himself out onto the roof, followed by Hungate, and they scrambled down the ladder at the forward end of the car. They stood for a moment, blinking against the noon glare, and filled their lungs with great drafts of clean, sweet air. After a week in their cramped and smelly cubbyhole, they were a grungy-looking pair. Covered with grime and a dusting of soot, their hair matted and filthy, the men gave off a gamy blend of odors. A swarm of flies buzzed around, inspecting them closer, attracted by the rancid mix of cowshit, stale sweat, and chewing tobacco.

Williams spotted them and hurried forward, hand outstretched. But, like the flies, he winded them some yards off. "Good to see you, Colter. How was the trip?"

"The cows made out real good." Colter smiled and pumped his hand a couple of times. "Wish I could say the same for us."

"Yeah, I see what you mean." Williams chuckled lightly and wrinkled his nose. "No offense, boys, but you smell like you've been sleepin' with a herd of goats."

Hungate squirted the fence with tobacco juice. "Hell, goats would've smelled like perfumed whores up beside them cows."

"Frank Williams"—Colter jerked his thumb at the big man—"this here's my partner, Emmet Hungate."

"Pleased to meet you," Williams said.

They shook hands, and Hungate nodded. "Same here."

The cattle buyer shifted around to a better position, slightly upwind. Smiling, he gestured back toward town. "This place ain't much for looks, but it's got a good hotel. Tub of hot water and a little soap'll fix you up real fast."

Hungate sniffed and worked his cud over to the off cheek. "Way I feel, it'd take a bucket of sand to get me scrubbed clean."

Williams was inclined to agree, but he merely smiled and looked back at Colter. "Think your cows came through okay then?"

"Lost less'n twenty head, best we can judge. Seems like there's always some damn fool that manages to get himself trampled. Could've been worse, though."

"Lots worse. I'd say your luck's runnin' strong." Williams motioned back to the pen. "Well, whatcha say we get 'em unloaded? Then we can see about gettin' you boys a bath."

As they turned, Colter caught movement out of the corner of his eye. Glancing back, he saw the stranger from Meade climb down from the caboose. Another man, dressed in range clothes, came forward from the station house to meet him. They shook hands, exchanging a few words, and then the second man fished out of his vest pocket what appeared to be a telegram. The one in town clothes studied it carefully a moment, made a comment of some sort, and tucked it away inside his coat. After a brief, one-sided discussion, with the stranger doing most of the talking, the men paused and looked off toward the cattle pen.

Colter returned their stare for a couple of seconds, then trailed along after Hungate and Williams. But his mind was still on that telegram. For some reason it lent an ominous note to the whole affair, and whatever message it spelled out, he felt sure it had to do with the herd of cows now being unloaded. All week the stranger had studiously avoided Hungate and himself at stops along the way. Yet at Kansas City, where the train crew had been switched, he had made no attempt to conceal sending a telegram of his own. Now, quite plainly, he had received an answer. Which left Colter more mystified than ever.

Wires had not yet been strung into No Man's Land, so it seemed unlikely that the message was from Covington. There was always a chance that the Colonel had stayed over in Meade, but that was a pretty slim possibility. Whatever Covington had planned, the idea of him loafing around Meade for a week seemed fairly remote. Much more likely was that the answering wire had come from a third party. Someone passing on final instructions.

But who?

The question was like a thorn in Colter's side. All the more so because there was no way of resolving it. Short of marching over and bracing the stranger, he hadn't the slightest inkling of what the telegram said or who it was from. Before, talking it over with Hungate as the train rattled northward, he had thrown out some wild guesses. None of them made a hell of a lot of sense, but they were at least something to hang his hat on. Now he was totally in the dark. Without a glimmering of what the bastards had up their sleeves. Except for one thing, perhaps: Somebody besides Covington was pulling the strings. Leastways at this end of the line. The telegram made that a damn strong likelihood. But knowing it did little to wipe away the cobwebs. If anything, it only added another snarl to an already impenetrable tangle.

Shunting it aside for the moment, he made his way forward and took a perch on one side of the loading chute. Williams straddled a fence rail on the other side, and as the cows emptied out of the cars they both commenced a running tally. The buyer's crew worked swiftly and with little lost motion, clearly men versed in the ways of unloading a herd and getting it settled with a minimum of fuss. Steers were goosed down the ramp until the pen was full; then the chute was closed. At that point a gate swung open on the far side, and the longhorns were hazed to a holding ground alongside a nearby stream. There riders milled them to a standstill, and the cows quickly fell to grazing. After being jammed for a week in stifling boxcars, the green grass and clear water was a lure they couldn't resist. The chance of them spooking and taking off in a wild run was all but eliminated by the slick operation of Williams's crew.

Colter observed all of this with the regard of one cowman watching another do his job, and do it well. The fact that these high-plains boys rode centerfire saddles and wore hats crowned like church steeples did nothing to lessen his esteem. They were smooth as butter. The equal of anything he had seen in Texas or elsewhere.

Slowly, though, he became aware of a far greater distraction. Between counting cows as they came down the chute, and watching the crew at work, he kept one eye peeled toward the station house. The stranger and his friend had gradually worked their way around the pen until they stood only a short distance from the gate. What with the dust and commotion, Colter couldn't be certain, but they seemed to be jotting notes in a small ledger of some sort. To what purpose he could only make an educated guess. But any lingering doubts about one thing had been erased completely. They were damned interested in every cow that came off the train.

Shortly before sundown the last of the steers was choused from the pen and Colter climbed down off the fence. He was bone-tired and covered with grit, and just then a hot bath sounded like a small slice of heaven. But, weary as he was, he couldn't shake a feeling that had grown steadily throughout the afternoon. Some gut instinct told him that he hadn't seen the last of this herd.

Williams and Hungate were waiting for him on the other side of the chute, and the contractor gave him a broad grin. "Them cows of yours are lots better'n I expected. Some of 'em a little scraggly, mebbe, but I was just tellin' Hungate we don't usually get the good stuff."

Hungate worked his jaws and splattered a car wheel dead center. "Nothin' but the best. That's our motto, ain't it, Buck?"

"Well, I'd have to say they was heavier a week ago, but, all things considered, I guess they held up pretty good."

"They'll tallow out between here and the reservation," Williams remarked. "What count did you make it?"

"Twenty-nine hundred and sixty-eight."

"That's funny." The contractor wet the tip of a stub pencil and made a quick check of his figures. After scratching his head, and double checking to be sure, he looked up. "I've got seventy-nine. And Hungate was lookin' over my shoulder the whole time."

Colter wasn't surprised. What with looking three directions at once, it was a wonder he'd come anywhere close. "I never argue with a higher tally. Unless you want to herd-count 'em, we'll let yours stand."

"Nope, I'm satisfied the way she sits. Now, if I calculate right, you've got a pile of simoleons comin' to you." Pausing, he took a peek at the figures on a piece of scratch paper. "Just to be exact, seventy-one thousand four hundred and ninety-six."

"Dollars?" Hungate blurted.

Colter looked a little dazed. "Sonovabitch!"

Williams had seen the same thunderstruck expression a hundred times over, but he couldn't resist a small chuckle. "Wanna check my figurin'?"

"Christ, no! I like the way you add."

"Fair enough. How'd you want it, cash or draft?"

"Tell you the truth, I hadn't given it much thought." Colter mulled it over a minute, but the dollar signs still had him dazzled. "Just gimme a couple of hundred in gold and the rest in a draft."

"Whatever suits. Let's walk on down to the

bank, and I'll have 'em fix it up any way you like."

Hungate and Colter fell in beside him, and they headed toward the depot. Beyond it was a town considerably larger than Benton, but neither of the cattlemen seemed to notice. They were near the end of the loading pen before Colter fully collected his wits.

"Say, it clean slipped my mind when you started tossin' around all them fancy figures. That's a good bunch of hands you've got. They work cows slick as anybody I ever saw."

"Yeah, I reckon they earn their keep. 'Course, it's not like they don't get plenty of practice. I've got the contract for a couple of different reservations, and that keeps us humpin' pretty regular."

"Mostly Sioux and Cheyenne, you said."

"Mostly. Sometimes I get the Crow contract too."

They paced along in silence for a minute, but Colter couldn't resist the temptation. "Seems like the government would want the tribes to raise herds of their own. Save a lot of money and teach 'em something useful to boot."

"Naw, hell, you can't trust Injuns to work at nothin'." Williams faltered and shot him a keen sidewise scrutiny. "Leastways that's what the Bureau says. Accordin' to Washington, it's better just to feed 'em and keep 'em happy."

"Some folks treat a mean dog the same way. Chain him up and throw him a piece of raw meat every once in a while."

Hungate snorted and gave him a queer look.

"Gawddamn, Buck, you sound like you've gone sweet on Injuns."

"All the same, he's got a point," Williams remarked. "There's no reason a red man can't learn a white man's tricks. Some day the Bureau'll wake up and put fellers like me out of business."

Just for a moment he thought Colter was going to take the bait, and he was congratulating himself on some nifty footwork. But the words were no sooner spoken than two men rounded the far end of the pen and strode briskly toward the station house. Colter's pace slowed, and he watched narrowly as they mounted the steps and disappeared inside.

After a moment he glanced over at Williams. "You notice them birds that just went in the depot?"

"Yeah, what about 'em?"

"They wouldn't happen to be Bureau men, would they?"

"Jesus H. Christ! I hope to tell you they're not. 'Course, I don't know the pilgrim, but the other one's Lem Tebbets. Cattle inspector from over Wyoming way."

"You talkin' about the Cattlemen's Association?"

"Same thing. Over there they call it the Stockgrowers' Association."

Colter's skin suddenly went hot and itchy. "Seems sort of queer, don't it? This Tebbets fellow being so far from home."

"Shit fire!" Williams snorted. "Cattle inspectors are like buzzards. They ain't got no home."

Hungate jumped in with an even spicier version, and Williams burst out laughing. But Colter was no longer listening.

Behind, he heard the clack of a telegraph key inside the depot.

FIFTEEN

Through the window Colter could barely make out lights. Darkness had already fallen, and the lamps in houses scattered around Meade glowed dimly. Seen from the grimy coach window, it was much the same as watching fireflies blink and fade along a distant river bank. The business section was black as pitch, lighted only by the hotel and a couple of saloons nearer the tracks. Like most country towns, Meade had little night life, and wasn't exactly a lodestar for the sporting crowd. People worked, lived the frugal life, and went to church on Sunday. All of which seemed pretty dull to a young cattleman who had just made his first killing.

Colter had few qualms about it, though. While Hungate had bellyached and sulked, they hadn't spent more than a couple of hours in either Omaha or Kansas City. Just long enough to change trains and be on their way. The big man was all for throwing a drunken wingding, hoorawing the city folks in real cowman fashion. But

Colter had turned thumbs down, caught up in some curious rush to again have his feet on home ground. Ruminating on it now as the train slowed outside Meade, he felt it had been the right choice. The wild life was for fiddlefoots like Hungate, men who lived fast with no thought of tomorrow. For him, though, there was a tomorrow—and Rachel—and that would be his celebration. Fulfilling the promise. Watching her eyes light up. Being with her, at last, under their own roof.

Until then a dull night in a hick town was nothing. Just a minor irritant, like gnats, that would pass with the darkness. An early start and a hard day's ride would finish it. Bring him once again to the Beaver and their secret place beneath the cottonwood and the soft, yielding warmth of Rachel. And, in time, the head of John Covington on a platter.

Ai! Then he would find his measure of content.

The train groaned to a halt, and Colter shook his partner awake. Denied his spree in the big city, Hungate had swilled the better part of a quart since early morning, and he was in a grumpy mood. Muttering sullenly to himself, he collected his gear and followed Colter toward the rear of the coach. They went through the door and emerged a moment later on the depot platform. The long ride had proved a dismal bore, particularly after Hungate crawled inside his bottle, and without a word they headed for the hotel. Just then a cushy bed and a good night's sleep seemed like an elixir they both needed.

"Colter!"

The word rang out like a pistol report. Wheeling about, they saw a man striding toward them, loose and easy, as if greeting old friends home from a trip. The air of elaborate ease didn't fool them, though. Not with that voice. He was past his prime, pushing forty, but he had all the earmarks of someone accustomed to having things his own way. Then something on his chest glittered, a flickering reflection from the lamp at the end of the platform, and they were no longer in doubt. He was wearing a tin star.

"Evenin'." He stopped a few feet away, unhurried but watchful. "I'm Jake Byrns. Sheriff of Meade County."

"Looks like you already know who I am." Colter jerked his chin at the big man. "This here's my partner, Emmet Hungate."

"Know him too," Byrns observed. "Had good descriptions on both you boys."

"Sheriff, I get the feelin' this isn't exactly social."

" 'Fraid you're right about that." The lawman pulled a folded paper from his shirt pocket. "Got a warrant for your arrest."

Colter gave him a wooden stare. "On what charge?"

"Cattle rustlin'."

"Horseshit!"

Hungate started to move, and suddenly found himself staring at a big black hole in the end of Byrns's pistol. The sheriff waited a moment, letting them get used to the idea, then smiled and holstered the Peacemaker in one slick motion.

"Don't get your nose out of joint, boys. I'm just here to serve the paper. Fact is, I won't even have to lock you up."

"How so?" Colter asked.

"'Cause a fellow name of Overton already posted your bond."

"Ed Overton?"

"That's the one."

"You sayin' he's mixed up in this too?"

"Clean up to his gizzard. 'Course, he come in peaceable, so the judge wasn't hardnosed about lettin' him make bond."

"What about Hungate?"

Byrns's gaze shifted to the big man. "Far as I know, he's in the clear. 'Less he gets another foolish notion to try jumpin' me."

Colter drew a long breath and let it go. "I guess there wouldn't be much need to askin' who brought the charges."

"Fellow name of Covington. Swore out the warrant as head of the Cattlemen's Association."

"Lousy good-for-nothin' bastard." Hungate's words were still slurred with whiskey. "He knows gawddamn well them cows wasn't rustled."

"Hell, it figures, Em. I should've seen it comin' a long ways back."

The lawman scratched his ear and looked interested. "Sounds like you figure they're tryin' to railroad you."

"That's the long and the short of it," Colter

agreed. "They'll play hell provin' it in court, though."

"Well, whatever they got, it was enough to get a warrant. Even sent a U.S. Marshal down to the Strip to bring Overton back."

"Where's Overton now?"

"Up at the hotel. We didn't rightly know which train you'd be on, so he asked me to tell you to meet him there."

"You mean I'm free to go?"

"Free as a bird. Leastways till the hearin'. That's tomorrow mornin' in Judge Ashland's court."

"Guess we'll see you there, then."

"Hope so. I'd hate to come lookin' for you." Byrns eyed him speculatively. "Been at this game twenty years, and I never yet seen the man that could outrun the law."

"Sheriff, the safest bet in town is that I'm not gonna start runnin'."

Colter nodded and turned back toward town, with Hungate ambling along beside him. The lawman walked to the end of the platform and kept them in sight as they strode hurriedly past darkened storefronts. When they entered the hotel he stood there a moment, hashing it around again in his mind. Wearing a badge paid good, but it had its drawbacks on occasion. Tonight being one of those times.

Somehow he felt like a first-class shitheel.

Colter left Hungate in the lobby signing the register. Taking the stairs two at a time, he hit the second floor and started down the hall. Almost immediately he heard a familiar outraged roar, and despite himself he had to chuckle. There had been no need to worm Overton's room number out of the clerk. The old man's raspy bellow carried like thunder, not to be contained by mere wood and wall plaster. Anybody that wasn't deaf knew exactly where he was staying. And most of what he was saying.

Halting before the door, he heard another voice, softer and somehow muted in the furious exchange. His knock brought deadened silence and, a moment later, the sound of lumbering footsteps crossing the room. Then the door flew open and Overton stood there glowering at him like a mad bull hooking at cobwebs. Colter managed a grin and stuck out his hand.

"This a private party, or can anybody join?"

"Goddamn, boy, you're a sight for sore eyes." The old man jerked him through the door and smote him across the back with a bristly paw. "I was beginnin' to think them sonsabitches had bushwacked you somewhere and left you to rot."

"Nope. Came through without a scratch. Leastways till I stepped off the train. Met a friend of yours there."

"Jake Byrns?"

Colter nodded. "Got a persuasive way about him."

"Damned if that ain't a fact. But he's better'n most lawdogs I've run acrost in my time." Overton suddenly remembered the man standing behind him and spun around. "Christ A'mighty, I almost forgot. Buck, this here's Harry Sample.

Treat him nice, 'cause he's about the only thing between us and a jail cell."

Sample extended a small, birdlike hand. "What he means, Mr. Colter, is that I'm a lawyer."

"And the best there is, too," Overton added. "Hired him the minute that smart-aleck deputy hauled me into town."

Colter had never been one to judge a man by appearances, but he found himself hoping there was more to Sample than met the eye. The attorney was a gnomish little man, scarcely larger than a circus midget. His face was wizened and seamed, almost as if it had been carved out of peach pit and shrunk a couple of notches tighter. But there was something about his eyes that tended to compensate for what he lacked in stature. A certain alert restlessness that mirrored a quick, searching mind. The look of a ferret or an otter, or a man who lived by his wits instead of his brawn. Colter had seen that same look among ancient ones of the Cheyenne, and he knew it for what it was. Devious and cunning and fast as a spring-steel trap. Some sudden sense of well-being surged through him, and he decided the old man had chosen wisely after all.

He let go of Sample's limp claw and smiled. "Glad you're on our side. I got an idea we're gonna need all the help we can get."

"That's precisely what I've been trying to tell Mr. Overton. Unfortunately, I haven't met with much success. He seems to be laboring under the opinion that a few well-placed loads of buckshot will resolve this whole issue."

Overton's mouth clamped in a bloodless line. "I don't know what I'm laboring under, but I'll tell you one thing. The first time I get Colonel John Covington in my sights, we'll be rid of this mess once and for all."

"Mr. Overton, you have a unique talent for missing the point entirely. Colonel Covington is nothing more than a figurehead, a vanguard, if you will. You're fighting an organization, not a man. And a very powerful organization, I might add."

The old man threw up his hands in disgust and turned to Colter. "Hear that? This fancy-talkin' little squirt is insultin' me with four-bit words and me payin' through the nose for it. If he wasn't so goddamned smart, I'd boot his ass right out the door."

"If he's so smart, why don't you listen to him?"

"Now just what the Sam Hill is that s'posed to mean?"

"Just what it sounds like. He's giving you the straight goods."

Overton's eyebrows came together in a quizzical squint. "I get the feelin' you know something we don't."

"Lots more'n you'll wanna hear. And none of it good, either."

Colter gave them a brief rundown on everything that had happened in the past two weeks. The stranger and the Wyoming cattle inspector, along with their nosy manner, were described in detail. But he reserved emphasis for what seemed the most crucial point: the series of telegrams that went humming back and forth across the wires, and that final deadly clicking as he walked away from the Valentine cattle pen.

"I didn't put it all together till I stepped off the train tonight. When the sheriff hit me with that warrant it was like my ears popped open. They've got us framed six ways to Sunday, and Covington's just a cog in the wheel. That's why I said Mr. Sample is right. Somebody's put together a damn big outfit, and it looks to me like they're set to put us away for a nice long stretch."

"Might makes right," Sample mused aloud.

"How's that?" Overton snapped.

"Nothing really. Just an old adage that never seems to go out of style. Essentially, what we're faced with, gentlemen, is an octopus. Its tentacles are far-reaching, and I suspect they have power in high places. They mean to crucify you in open court. Right out in public, where you will serve as an object lesson for anyone else who might be tempted to challenge them."

The old man gave him an owlish frown. "You mind breakin' that down into plain English?"

"Not at all," Sample countered. "Bluntly stated, you've got your ass between a rock and a hard spot."

Colter grunted and let out his breath between clenched teeth. The lawyer might be a runt, but he packed a wallop. Which was more than likely the very thing they needed.

Somebody that knew how to hit below the belt.

SIXTEEN

The courtroom was curiously crowded. Word of the hearing had apparently circulated around, and though Meade County was mostly farm country, there were several good-sized ranches south of town. Spectators had come early to stake out the best seats, and from the looks of their garb, almost everyone present was a cattleman. Evidently the Association had billed the affair as an extravaganza of sorts. Law-abiding ranchers versus night-riding rustlers. Not unlike ancient days, when well-heeled sports fed people to the lions, this chummy little gathering had come to watch the Association devour a couple of troublemakers.

Harry Sample stalked in as if he had just foreclosed the mortgage on the courthouse. Bustling down the aisle, with Colter and Overton at his heels, he whisked through the bar gate and moved directly to the defense table. Sample motioned his clients to their seats and began pulling legal-looking documents from a battered leather briefcase. Overton and Colter exchanged puzzled glances and shifted uncomfortably in their chairs. They were new to this game, but as they watched Sample busily shuffling papers it slowly dawned on them that he was giving a performance. The diminutive lawyer had absolutely nothing pertaining to the case, yet anyone looking on would have suspected otherwise. From his crisp manner and the sheaf of documents, he gave the impression of a man who had things well under control.

Colter felt a hand on his shoulder, and turned to find Hungate seated in the front pew, just across the railing. The big man had wedged out a place for himself among the early birds, and they seemed none too happy that he had joined them. Hungate leaned forward, ignoring the hostile looks, and rested his arms on the railing.

"Buck, this gawddamned place looks like a circus. Where'd all these rubbernecks come from?"

"Beats the hell out of me. Guess they heard there was a dog fight being held and they just couldn't stay away."

"You notice anything funny about 'em? Like mebbe they forgot to scrape the cowshit off their boots."

"Yeah, I've got an idea the Association called out the troops." Colter's gaze drifted over the crowd a moment, then swung back. "What're you doing here, anyway? I thought you were gonna stick around the hotel and get rid of that hangover."

Hungate's eyes were bloodshot, and he looked

a little queasy. "Hell, so I tied one on. Seemed like a good night for it. Ain't ever' day my pardner gets arrested, y'know."

"Maybe so. But you're still sort of green around the gills."

"Naw, I'm fine. Just had myself a little hair of the dog that bit me. Gimme another stiff one and I could whip my weight in wildcats."

"Way things are shapin' up, you might get the chance. This bunch looks about as friendly as a pack of vultures."

Colter suddenly stopped talking, and his backbone went stiff as a poker. A hush fell over the courtroom, and people started craning their necks for a better look as two men marched down the aisle. The one in the lead was smartly tailored, hair slicked back, and carried a fancy hand-tooled briefcase. Behind him, shoulders squared back and staring straight ahead, was John Covington. They came through the bar gate, proceeded to the prosecution table, and seated themselves. Opening his briefcase, the spiffy dresser went into the paper-shuffling routine, which seemed to be standard practice for lawyers.

Harry Sample reared back like a gamecock sizing up an adversary, and a slight scowl crept over his features. Then, quite abruptly, he sat down and gave his clients a disturbed look. "Gentlemen, I'm afraid we're in more trouble then even I suspected."

"What're you gettin' at?" Overton asked.

"The man with Covington is George Cowan.

He's the attorney for the Fort Worth Cattlemen's Association."

Colter and Overton shot a quick glance toward the prosecution table. They caught Covington studying them with icy detachment, but when he saw them staring back, his expression changed to a mocking smirk. Colter became aware that Sample was watching the byplay, and he turned back to the little lawyer.

"Covington looks like he just swallowed the canary."

"With good reason. George Cowan is shrewd, ruthless, and utterly without principle. He commands a high fee, and the Association gets its money's worth."

"Spell that out a little bit, will you?" Overton dug at his ear with a horny finger. "What's him being here got to do with anything?"

"Quite obviously the Association has decided to drag out its heavy artillery." Sample stacked his papers in a neat pile, as if the need for display had passed. "We can assume that they pulled some strings and had Cowan appointed prosecuting attorney. Perhaps the significance of that will become apparent if I tell you that Cowan has never lost a case involving the Association."

He fished out his watch, clicked open the case, and consulted the time. After a moment he glanced up. "So you see, Mr. Colter, our friend Colonel Covington has every reason to look smug."

Overton huffed and started a question just as the rear door of the courtroom swung open. The bailiff walked to a position in front of the bench, ordered the spectators to their feet, and declared court in session. Judge Fred Ashland meanwhile made his way to the bench, seated himself, and, with the preliminaries out of the way, called the court to order.

"Is the prosecution ready?"

"Ready, Your Honor," Cowan replied.

"Defense?"

Sample stood and nodded in the affirmative. "The defense is also prepared, Your Honor."

"You gentlemen understand that this is merely a hearing? To determine whether or not the accused should be bound over for trial." The judge waited for a response from both lawyers, then folded his hands over his stomach and settled back. "Very well, Mr. Cowan, you may proceed for the prosecution."

George Cowan came slowly to his feet, paused for a moment of reflection, then walked to the front of the table. "May it please the court, the prosecution intends to prove that the accused, Edward Overton and Buck Colter, did willfully and maliciously appropriate livestock belonging to fellow ranchers and at a later date sell the livestock in question to a Federal beef contractor."

With the precise care of a stonemason laying brick, Cowan began to outline his case step by step. Over the next hour Wash Sealy and reps from various spreads along the Beaver were called to the stand. They testified that Overton and Colter had gathered cows belonging to other outfits during the early fall roundup and claimed them as their own. Afterward Covington swore under oath that he had seen this very same stock loaded on a train by the accused in Meade. Finally, Cowan presented a sworn deposition from Sam Lyons, cattle inspector for the Dodge City Stockgrowers' Association, which told of some two hundred cows bearing the wrong brands being unloaded in Valentine, Nebraska.

Cowan handed the deposition to the bailiff, stepped back, and hooked his thumbs in his vest pockets. "Your Honor, Mr. Lyons is at this very moment gathering evidence to further substantiate these charges, and we beg the court's indulgence that he was unable to testify in person here today. However, the prosecution believes the evidence presented to be massive and overwhelming, and we request that the accused be remanded for trial at the earliest possible date. I thank you."

Judge Ashland waited for Cowan to resume his seat, then turned to the defense table. "Mr. Sample, you may proceed for the defense."

Harry Sample rose, his face grave and thoughtful, and moved to the center of the courtroom. Surprisingly, when he began to speak, his voice was husky and impassioned, with a kind of smothered wrath.

"Your Honor, without resorting to invective, I am forced to say that the prosecution has presented us with a hodgepodge of testimony, but nothing of substance. We are dealing in a matter of one man's word against another, and I think it is high time the court heard the truth. I call Edward Overton to the stand."

Overton made a bad witness, blustering, outraged, his testimony larded with profanity. Sample finished with him as quickly as possible and summoned Colter to the stand. The younger man handled himself much better, allowing the lawyer to lead him point by point through the story. His testimony was straightforward, without noticeable rancor, and told with little or no garnishment. Sample excused him only after lengthy and meticulous questioning. He hesitated, waiting for Colter to take his seat, and then walked to the front of the bench.

"If it please the court, I enter a motion at this time that the charges against my clients be dismissed on all counts. The prosecution has not only failed to present a prima-facie case but, more significantly, they appear singularly reluctant to produce their key witness. The one man whose testimony is crucial to their argument. I refer specifically to Mr. Sam Lyons, the Association inspector. That the prosecution has not produced him, Your Honor, is highly suspect, and constitutes grounds for dismissal of these heinous charges. I so request."

Sample scarcely had time to return to his seat before the judge straightened and, in a dry monotone, rendered his decision. "The court finds that sufficient evidence exists to warrant a full disclosure of the facts. The defendants will be bound over for trial two weeks from this date. And please, Mr. Sample, no motions for a continuance. I believe two weeks is entirely adequate for you to prepare your case. However, in view of the substantial bond posted, I will allow the defendants to remain free during the interim."

Judge Ashland banged the gavel and rose ponderously to his feet. "This hearing stands adjourned."

The hotel room was thick with smoke from Colter's cigarettes and the lawyer's pipe. Overton paced the floor like a caged bear, swearing and muttering and generally working himself into a towering rage. Sample sucked on his pipe, lost in thought, oblivious to the old man's fiery tirade.

"I'll say it again, goddammit. It was fixed. Right from scratch. Those connivin' egg-suckin' sonsabitches bought that judge just like you'd buy a tin of lard. Slimy bastard rattled off that verdict like he'd been in the back room practicin' it since breakfast. Probably had, too. That or countin' his money."

"Ed, why don't you simmer down?" Colter ground out his cigarette and heaved a huge sigh. "All this hollerin' of yours is gettin' us no place fast."

"Now is that a fact? Lemme tell you something, boy. Where we're gettin' is strung up by the short hairs. Way I see it, we've only got two ways to go—put a gun to Covington's head and make him start talkin', or take off runnin' like scalded cats. Otherwise, we're gonna get free room and board for about ten years. You just chew on that for a minute."

Sample drifted back out of his fog. "That is precisely what they want you to do."

"Come again," Overton growled.

"They want you to run. Then they could put a price on your head and have you legally executed by some bounty hunter. From their standpoint, that would be an even better object lesson than sending you to prison."

"Then why didn't they just kill us to start with?" Colter inquired.

"I suspect it has to do with last summer's meeting in Denver. This new alliance of all cattlemen's associations. The goals haven't changed, but they're trying to do it in a respectable manner. Political clout and manipulation of the legal machinery rather than violence. Of course, if you run, then killing you becomes perfectly legal."

"So what do we do, roll over and play dead?"

"Not just yet. I've been thinking that a trip to Nebraska is in order."

Overton halted, plainly dumbfounded. "Nebraska!"

"Gentlemen, in the parlance of the gambling fraternity, you're playing against a cold deck. What we need are some depositions of our own. Specifically, from your contractor friend and his crew. That should do it very nicely, I'd think."

Sample's eyes brightened with a crafty look. After a moment he chuckled, and with the stem of his pipe scribed a cross motion in the air.

"Tit for tat."

SEVENTEEN

It was the Geese Going Moon, and the cottonwoods gave off bright flurries of crimsoned gold. Colter had never really rid himself of such thoughts. Certain things clung to him still, and were better expressed in Cheyenne. The Quakers had taught him that when the geese winged southward it was October, but the word somehow fell short of the earth and its creatures. When the plains went tawny, and hoarfrost came at night to the land, there was a magic that touched something deep inside him. The blood of the True People and the old ways and a time that was no more. Whites could call it whatever they wanted, but back in that secret little crannny reserved only to himself, it would forever remain the Geese Going Moon.

Grunting, he shook himself like a sleepy dog, and feathered the sorrel with his spurs. Such thoughts were better set aside, for a time when he had less on his mind. Tonight he would see Rachel—after being apart nearly a month—and he had a pretty fair hunch what to expect for a homecoming present. She had fire and spirit, and a hunger to match his own, and he figured to be weaker in the knees when he rode away than when he arrived.

Turning off from the Beaver, he reined into the lane leading to the Goddard homestead. The moon was out, and the rutted path was bathed in a soft, fuzzy glow. If Overton hadn't slowed him down, he would have made it by suppertime, but the old man refused to be hurried. Less than an hour past, he'd left Overton and Hungate back on the river trail and ridden on ahead. They had joshed him a good bit and thrown in a few ribald remarks about his impatience. But he took it as a good sign that they could joke when there was so little to joke about.

The ride south from Meade had been a time of reflection, long on thought and short on talk. Overton had quit throwing off sparks and finally given himself over to some serious rumination. Harry Sample's trip to Nebraska had gradually had a sobering effect on his smoky tirades. That the little lawyer would undertake such a journey spoke eloquently of the fix they found themselves in just now. Earlier that afternoon, with several miles of silence behind them, the old man had laid it out neat and pithy.

They were up to their necks and sinking fast.

Unless Sample returned with a satchelful of evidence, they were prime candidates for a ball and chain. The chute had been greased, and if the Association ever pushed them over the edge, they were goners for sure. The hell of it was, their hands were tied. They couldn't fight and they couldn't run. They could only wait for the pint-sized attorney to return.

And hope.

Colter rode into the yard and made straight for the barn. The cider-colored glow of a lamp in the parlor window was inviting, but he resisted the urge to rush inside. Six years in the saddle had taught him that a man looked to his horse first, for the plains was no place to be caught on foot. Afterward, in whatever time remained, a man could rest easy and look to his own needs.

Hurriedly he unsaddled, watered the sorrel, and pitched down a forkload of hay. Batting around in the darkened barn, he finally located an empty towsack, and spent a few minutes rubbing the gelding down. But as for himself, there wasn't much be could do besides slap the dust from his clothes and slick his hair back a bit. Crossing the yard, it came to him that, taken as a pair, the horse was probably the better-looking. And doubtless smelled better, too.

Joe Goddard opened the door to his knock and, after a moment of slack-jawed astonishment, broke out in a whooping yell. "Great jumpin' jehosophat! C'mon in this house, boy. We'd just about give you up for lost."

The old man pulled him through the doorway and let go with a crackling laugh. "Rachel! Mother! Looka here who showed up. It's Buck!"

Rachel flew across the parlor and threw herself into his arms. Tears were streaming down her cheeks, and she smothered him with wet, salty kisses. Sarah Goddard and the girls were only a step behind, and the whole family stood around grinning and reaching out to touch him with affectionate pats. Finally Rachel planted one square on his lips and held it a long time. Then she let go with a loud smacking sound and stood back, wrinkling her forehead in a mock frown.

"Land's sakes, Buck Colter, don't you ever do that again. I've been worried nearly out of my mind. First we heard you were arrested and then that you were free and then somebody said you'd been locked up. We didn't know who to believe, and I was just frantic. Ask Mama. I thought I was going to swell up and die. Truly, I did."

"She's right, boy." Goddard smote him across the back, raising a little puff of dust. "We thought you was a gone goose. There's talk all over town that the Association fixed your wagon permanent."

Colter passed it off with a wave of his hand. "They tried, but it didn't work out just the way they wanted."

"You're not runnin' from the law, are you?" Goddard darted a quick glance at the window. "Listen, I got a place back up the creek where you could hide out and God hisself couldn't find you."

"That's right!" Rachel blurted. "Where Pa runs his still. Oh, Buck, it's perfect. They'd never find you in a hundred years."

"Whoa back, everybody." Colter grinned and warded them off with outstretched palms. "I'm free as a bird. Leastways for the time being. They lemme out on bond, and we don't go to trial for two weeks."

"Trial!" Goddard boomed. "Boy, are you daft? You can't beat 'em in no court. Homesteaders has already learned that the hard way."

"Joe Goddard, you stop that right now." The old lady gave him a withering look. "Can't you see he's all tuckered out? Gracious sakes alive, he likely half starved, and you standing there shouting nonsense at him." She glanced around at Colter. "Now, Buck, don't you try to act polite. Couldn't you eat something if I laid out a table?"

"Yes, ma'am, I believe I surely could. 'Bout the only thing between my belt buckle and my backbone is a big grumblin' noise."

They all broke out laughing and Sarah Goddard whisked off toward the kitchen. Rachel grabbed one arm and the girls took the other, and they hustled him along after her. The old man brought up the rear, and they trooped into the kitchen with May giggling and Bertha Lou grinning like a filly eating briars. The Goddards believed that a full stomach cured all ills, and they never allowed life's miseries to intrude on the pleasures of a hearty meal. Colter was seated at the head of the table, and the rest of the family pulled up chairs and commenced jabbering in what looked to be a marathon of sorts. Just so it was amusing, or didn't reflect on the worries of the day, they seemed to spout anything that came into their heads. Outclassed and outnumbered, Colter merely smiled and looked on, reminded again that Rachel's gift for chatter was simply another sprig on the family tree.

Sarah Goddard proceeded to shove plates and mugs and pitchers in front of him with dizzying speed. Cold fried chicken and a huge glop of blackeyed peas and sowbelly. Leftover biscuits and churned butter and fancy preserves. Thick syrupy coffee laced with fresh cream. And finally a mound of dried-apple cobbler with a glass of buttermilk the size of a fishbowl.

Colter ate it all, listening and nodding, methodically working his way through each dish without uttering a single word. The Goddards jabbered on like a flock of twittering birds, watching with enormous relish as he devoured everything set before him. They enjoyed feeding others almost as much as they enjoyed feeding themselves, and every member of the family was pleasured by the load he stoked away.

With the last dish scraped clean and his belly distended, Colter finally called it quits. Tilting back in his chair, he hauled out the makings and started building himself a smoke. The first puff had the taste of paradise about it, and he lounged back with the groggy contentment of a gorged cat. The Goddards stopped talking all of a sudden, glancing at one another with quick little smiles and knowing looks. Then they waited, watching him closely, as if they had run dry of words the moment he lit his cigarette. When Sarah Goddard came to the table and took a seat, he finally understood. It was something on the order of a ritual, not too different from the way a visitor would have been treated in a Cheyenne lodge. The family had entertained him throughout the meal, and now, as a guest with important news, he was expected to satisfy their curiosity.

Colter began to talk, haltingly at first, but slowly he warmed to the story. After that the words came easier, and step by step he described the finely spun web that had ended with his arrest and the courtroom hearing. Rachel and her mother were appalled, and it showed in their faces. The old man simply nodded from time to time, sucking stolidly on a cold pipe, and the girls listened in oval-eyed fascination. They were simple people, accustomed to the blunt and sometimes brutal ways of cattlemen, and this tale of intrigue and subterfuge held them spellbound. When Colter came at last to the end, they just sat there, staring at him in dazed wonder.

After a while Goddard blinked and cleared his throat. "Well, there's one thing for plumb certain. We'll back you clean to the hilt, any way we can, and so'll ever' homesteader in the Strip. They've give us farmers a hard way to go, and most likely it'll get harder yet. If you was of a mind, I don't reckon you'd have any trouble raisin' a small army to help you fight 'em."

"That wouldn't do much but get a lot of people killed. Especially with them havin' your folks outnumbered so bad." Colter took a pull on his cigarette, reflecting back on something the little lawyer had said. "The thing we've got to do is beat 'em at their own game. Whip 'em in court legal like. Then everybody'll see 'em for what they are, and things'll stop being so one-sided. Maybe we'll get some law for the little fellow, instead of the courts and everything being rigged to protect the big dog."

The statement was met with doubtful silence, and after a few seconds he smiled wryly. "We mightn't beat 'em, but you can bet money on one thing. Before it's done with, they're gonna know they've been in a fight."

Sarah Goddard climbed to her feet and began clearing the table. But as she took the buttermilk pitcher, she paused and looked him straight in the eye. "Buck, you and Rachel haven't stood up with the preacher yet, but you're one of the family just the same. That's the way us Goddards are. Don't be so proud that you wouldn't ask for help if you need it. That's what family is for."

She turned away before he could frame a reply, and, as if nothing unusual had happened, the girls began chattering right where they had left off earlier. The old man shoved his chair back and headed for the parlor, a big grin plastered across his face. Tagging along behind Rachel and the girls, Colter got the feeling he had just been adopted into a clan of some sort. A maternal clan at that.

Again, it struck him as not so different from the Cheyenne.

Later, after the others had retired for the night, he and Rachel went for a walk. They were crossing the yard when she suddenly stopped and looked up at him. The moonlight did something nice to her eyes, but the set of her jaw was dead serious.

"I don't suppose you'd consider giving in. I mean, if you quit buying cows and went back to work as a hand, the Association would most likely forget this whole business."

Colter regarded her impassively for a moment, then shook his head. "Guess not. I saw a fellow turn the other cheek one time. All it got him was two black eyes instead of one."

She came up on tiptoe and kissed him. "I wouldn't have it any other way. If you say fight, then we'll fight. I just wanted to hear you say it."

He chuckled, pleasured again by her spirit and the feisty gleam in her eye. They stood there grinning at each other for a second; then he took her hand and started toward the creek. Rachel dug in her heels and yanked him back. Surprised, he came about as she stepped forward and snuggled close to his chest.

"Buck, honey, the ground's awful cold down at the creek."

"Yeah, I guess it is." He puzzled on it a moment, then smiled. "Bet it wouldn't be cold at all up in the hayloft."

She gave him a vixenish look and giggled softly. "You wicked devil. I just knew you'd think of something. But, Lordy me, won't I be glad when you make an honest woman of me."

The sorrel whickered when they entered the barn, and craned its head around to watch as Colter helped her climb the ladder. Then they disappeared into the loft, and the horse again dozed off in a peaceful sleep. The barn went still

once more, and the gentle rustlings from overhead disturbed nothing. Through a crack in the
roof the Geese Going Moon sprinkled flecks of
gold across the sweet-scented hay.

EIGHTEEN

Colter didn't like the looks of the jury: four ranchers from outside Meade, three cowhands, and five merchants and tradesmen from the town itself. They kept darting sidewise glances at him and Overton, as if the Devil and his first cousin had been hauled in on charges of molesting old ladies. Under their scrutiny the young cattleman felt a long way from home, and down in the pit of his belly a nest of worms had gone to work on his vitals. It was like Judgment Day the Quakers had always harped about. Only instead of some misty afterlife, it was being held in the here-and-now.

Seated beside him, Harry Sample studied the jury with an equally jaundiced eye. He was watching their reaction as the prosecutor questioned Wash Sealy, and what he saw was something less than reassuring. The jury members were raptly attentive, soaking up every word, and it was all too apparent that they wanted to believe the Circle C foreman's story. Whole truth, half truth, or lie, they had come into court prepared to accept whatever tale the prosecution cared to weave.

Yet there was nothing the little lawyer could do to change it now. The day before, when the jury was being selected, he had exhausted his peremptory challenges in short order. Not a farmer or homesteader or common working man in the bunch. Nor was there any doubts as to the reason. The Association had pulled all the right strings, and every member of the panel was obligated to it in one fashion or another. Even the merchants knew what would happen to their steady trade if they failed to vote the verdict dictated by the Association.

Thinking about it now, Sample was reminded that the wheels of justice ground finely, if not always fairly. Sometimes pulverizing the lives of innocent men in the process. His one remaining hope was that he could punch some large and rather unsavory holes in the prosecution's case. Riddle it so thoroughly that not even a packed jury would have the nerve to bring in a guilty verdict.

George Cowan had led Wash Sealy through his testimony like a trained seal, and it was a convincing performance. Turning from the witness chair, he strode confidently back to the prosecution table.

"That's all I have for this witness, Your Honor."

Judge Ashland cleared his throat. "Cross-examine, Mr. Sample?"

Sample rose and slowly approached the witness box. As though distracted, he shuffled a batch of papers in his hand and studied each intently. Mumbling something to himself, he halted and gave Sealy a disarming smile.

"Mr. Sealy, I have only a few questions for you. Just a couple of points that puzzle me somewhat, and I thought you might be able to clarify things a bit."

The foreman just stared at him, alert and plainly suspicious.

"Well now, suppose we begin, Mr. Sealy. I believe you testified that you have been working cows for close to twenty years. Is that correct?"

"That's what I said."

"And I believe the prosecution was at some pains to qualify you an expert on steers and horses and the workings of a ranch. In other words, there aren't many men who could teach you what's what with cows."

Sealy sat up a little straighter and allowed himself a smile. "I ain't one to brag, but I don't reckon anybody'd try learnin' me to suck eggs."

Several of the jurors snickered, and Sample himself chuckled appreciatively. "I dare say they wouldn't, Mr. Sealy. Now, I believe you further testified that on the day in question this past August, you discovered a Circle C steer being driven to the trail herd of the accused?"

"I did, for a fact."

"And one of the accused, Mr. Colter, threatened you and drove you away from the roundup?"

"That's about the gist of it."

"Now think carefully on this next question,

Mr. Sealy. Are you absolutely certain that the steer you saw had been branded over before it reached the trail herd?"

" 'Course I am. I seen it with my own eyes, didn't I?"

"Good. I just wanted you to be sure. Perhaps we can move now to the point that puzzles me."

Sample held up two pieces of paper, showing them first to the judge, then to Sealy, and finally to the jury. In bold, heavy ink a brand had been drawn on each piece of paper. One bore the marking © and the second was imprinted with ↯C.

"Mr. Sealy, I'm somewhat of an ignoramus concerning cows and brands and things of that sort. As an expert, I wonder if you would mind explaining to me—and the jury—exactly how a man would go about transforming a Circle C into a Broken Arrow C?"

The foreman's jaw clicked shut and he just sat there, staring at the brands.

"Any suggestions on how it was done, Mr. Sealy?"

A long moment passed, and Sealy failed to respond. Sample strolled to the jury box, laid the papers on the rail, and casually walked off toward the defense table.

"Your Honor, it appears that the witness is as confused as everyone else on this point. The answer is rather obvious, at any rate. No further questions."

Sealy was excused, and John Covington followed him to the stand. The cattleman made a somewhat better witness, speaking forcefully and with just the right shade of restrained anger. Sample was unable to shake his story on cross-examination, settling for an admission that the Association could have acted long before it did. Covington weasled a bit on the issue, limply stating that it was easier to prove rustling if the thief was caught selling the cows.

The prosecution's next witness was Sam Lyons, cattle inspector for the Dodge City Stock-growers' Association. Overton and Colter both stiffened as Lyons made his way to the stand. This was the stranger. The one who had followed their herd from Kansas to Nebraska, and heretofore had been heard from only in a highly damaging deposition.

Lyons told a straightforward story, avoiding any nonsense about running irons. He had seen the herd loaded in Meade and unloaded in Valentine, and he testified that close to two hundred steers bore the brands of cattlemen in No Man's Land. As proof he offered a tally book showing the brands in question, and further testified that an inspector from the Wyoming Association had assisted him in checking the cattle as they were unloaded. Prosecutor Cowan immediately produced a deposition from the Wyoming inspector supporting Lyons's story and had it admitted as evidence.

The stunner came with Cowan's last question. "Mr. Lyons, have you any corroborative evidence that the steers in question were actually sold to the Rosebud Indian reservation?"

"I have," Lyons stated emphatically. From the back of the tally book he pulled a small square of dried cowhide. On it was the Box T brand, Overton's neighbor to the east. "This was cut from a steer killed by a Sioux Indian on ration day at the agency. The incident occurred exactly eleven days ago, and is further verified by the Wyoming inspector in his deposition. He was present, and saw me pay the Indian two bits for this piece of hide."

Cowan walked back to his chair with elaborate ease, then turned and smiled at Sample. "Your witness, counselor."

The defense attorney held a hurried conference with his clients, but both Colter and Overton appeared dumbfounded by the strip of cowhide. Sample smiled reassuringly and climbed to his feet, gathering another batch of papers. Lyons was an old hand at courtroom testimony, and the little lawyer saw nothing to be gained in a devious approach. He walked briskly to the witness box and thrust the papers under Lyons's nose.

"Mr. Lyons, your testimony hardly bears repeating. I'm wondering, though, how you can explain to this court and this jury that I hold in my hand sworn depositions from Frank Williams, the beef contractor, and ten of his cowhands—"

"Objection!" Cowan thundered.

"—depositions, Mr. Lyons, which swear that the steers in that herd bore only the brands of the Slash O and the Broken Arrow C."

"Objection!" Cowan trumpeted again. "These so-called depositions haven't even been introduced as evidence. I submit to the court that this is highly irregular conduct on the part of defense counsel."

"Sustained," intoned Judge Ashland. "Watch yourself, Mr. Sample."

Sample went through the formality of submitting the documents, watching the judge scan them, and at last hearing the depositions entered as evidence. With that accomplished, he returned to the witness stand.

"Now, Mr. Lyons, we're waiting for your explanation."

"Well, offhand, I'd say somebody was lyin'. Since most cattle buyers are crooked as a dog's hind leg, and everybody knows it, there's not much trick to figure out who's tellin' the truth."

"Isn't it a fact, Mr. Lyons, that stockgrowers' associations across the West work together to keep small ranchers such as my clients from expanding their operations?"

"Objection," Cowan snapped. "Calls for an opinion."

"Sustained. Jury will disregard the last question."

"Isn't it also a fact, Mr. Lyons, that this whole shoddy affair consists of charges trumped up by the Association to ruin my clients?"

"Objection." Cowan threw his hands up in disgust. "Argumentative."

"Sustained." Judge Ashland peered over his glasses at the defense attorney. "You're skating on thin ice, Mr. Sample."

Sample scarcely bothered acknowledging the rebuff. "I have but one last question, Mr. Lyons. How is it that you had a Wyoming cattle inspector certify the origin of this piece of cowhide instead of the Rosebud Indian Agent? Could it be that this strip of hide was taken not from a Box T steer in Dakota but from a Box T steer in No Man's Land? Isn't that the whole truth, Mr. Lyons?"

Cowan jumped to his feet, but Sample waved him off and stalked away from the witness stand. "I have no further questions of this witness, Your Honor."

The prosecution rested its case, and Sample went through the motions of presenting a defense. Overton and Colter and Hungate were called to the stand, and gave their version of what had transpired from the Beaver to the cattle pens in Valentine. But it was a futile effort at best. The jury looked bored, and George Cowan's cross-examination was little more than a formality. The verdict was a foregone conclusion, and everyone in the courtroom knew it. After final summations, Judge Ashland charged the jury, and the twelve men filed through a door at the back of the room.

Sample slumped wearily into his chair and motioned his clients to take a seat. "Gentlemen, I regret to say you might as well stay put. The way those jurors looked, you won't even have time for a smoke."

"That bad?" Overton growled.

"Cut and dried." The little lawyer sighed. "The Association had us in a hammerlock from the start. Lyons and his piece of cowhide merely nailed it down tight. I suggest you prepare yourselves for the worst."

"We never had a chance, did we?" Colter's voice was low and raspy, and his fists clenched so tight his knuckles went white. "They had it rigged from the minute we trailed that herd across the Beaver."

Sample gave him a speculative look, alerted suddenly that the younger man's soft-spoken manner belied a simmering rage. "Buck, don't try anything foolish. Not at this point. We still have an appeal, and if necessary we can carry it all the way to the Supreme Court."

"Yeah, sure. And if that don't work, whatta we do then—start prayin'?"

"It's a thought," Sample admitted. "Right now we could use all the help we can get."

Less than five minutes later the rear door opened and the jurors filed back into their seats. Judge Ashland made it to the bench about the same time and banged the gavel for order.

"Gentlemen of the jury, have you reached a verdict?"

The jury foreman rose. "We have, Your Honor."

"Defendants will rise." The judge waited for Overton and Colter to stand, then glanced back at the foreman. "How do you find?"

"We find 'em guilty as hell, Judge. On all counts."

The judge appeared something less than surprised. "Edward Overton and Buck Colter, you have been found guilty of rustling cows. I hereby remand you to the custody of the sheriff. Sentencing to be held tomorrow morning at ten o'clock. This court stands adjourned."

It was over before Colter had time to take a deep breath. Somewhat dazed by the speedy dispatch of justice, he turned and froze dead still. Sheriff Jake Byrns was standing there, one hand on the butt of his pistol and the other holding a set of manacles.

"S'pose you fellers just hold out your wrists and we'll see how these bracelets fit."

This time he wasn't smiling.

NINETEEN

The sound kept returning throughout the night. A cell door clanging shut. Like the jaws of a steel trap closing hungrily in cold embrace. It jarred him awake, beading his forehead with sweat, and he slept only in bits and snatches. With false dawn he was up and pacing, moving around the cell with the restless fury of a caged wolf. The more he stalked, the greater became his rage. He was a man born to vast spaces and bright skies, with the plains breeze and the warm sun and the green earth as his rightful domain. A free man to come and go and do as he would. Not some obedient dog to be whipped into submission and locked away in a stinking cage.

The cell was a small steel box, separated from other cells on either side by bars set into mortared stone. He prowled back and forth with a fierce, mounting desperation. Trapped, just as surely as if he had been entombed alive in a vault of steel. His eyes were shot through with flecks of red and fiery gold, and his jaws were clapped shut in a grim line. Silently he cursed the men who had put him there, and the courts, and most of all he cursed himself. For it was he alone who had chosen the white man's road. Set himself on a path that led straight as a string to this grungy jail. A pesthole that had about it the lingering reek of urine and sweat and rancid vomit.

All of a sudden he stopped pacing.

This was only the first night. The beginning. They meant to lock him away for five years. Ten. Maybe more. Hold him in a cage, shackled with chains, like some wild beast that had no place among civilized men.

Then, his mind reeling, he was struck by another thought. Covington would go free while he rotted in some dank prison cell. The man who had put him here—the Pony Soldier leader who murdered women and children—would live and prosper. The long wait for revenge, biding his time with spidery patience for the past three years, would have been in vain. A washout. Just another cipher in the list of naughts his life had become. Once the prison gates slammed shut behind him there would be nothing. Not Rachel. Not the ranch. And, perhaps more loathsome than all the rest, not a chance in hell of killing John Covington.

He sat down on the lumpy cot and started to think.

With sunrise Overton came awake in the next cell and spent several grunting minutes squatting over his slop jar. By then Colter was composed and wooden-faced. Some inner discipline, a carryover from the training of his youth, had enabled him to take a steely grip on the smoldering rage. He chatted with the old man, calm and outwardly at ease, lounging back on his cot with the lithe grace of a sleepy cat. But his words were stilted, little more than a mechanical response, for his mind focused on a single thought. What in the past quarter-hour had become a raw and suppurating obsession.

Somehow he meant to escape.

Shortly after they had been served breakfast—a plate of fried mush washed down with bitter coffee—the cellblock door swung open. Emmet Hungate waltzed through with a toothy grin and a quart of whiskey. Behind him, a deputy remained in the doorway, pistol drawn and cocked, watching the big man's every move with a beady-eyed squint.

"Mornin', gents." Hungate seemed chipper as a frisky pup. "How's life in the cooler?"

Overton looked thoroughly nonplused, as if the words hadn't quite registered, and Colter's astonishment was only slightly less apparent. He managed a bemused smile and came off the cot, moving to the cell door.

"Em, how in Chrissakes did you get in here?"

"Hell, weren't nothin' to it. Just soft-soaped the sheriff a little bit and he damn near gimme the keys to this place. Y'know, for a lawdog he ain't a bad sort a-tall. Regular square shooter."

"Yeah, but you must've told him something. They just don't throw open the doors everytime some slick talker walks in off the street."

"Sure I told him somethin'." Hungate's grin

widened, and he held up the quart. "Told him any man headed for the rockpile deserved a last swig of redeye. That's what I meant about him bein' a square shooter. Said he figured you fellers could stand a little cheerin' up before they hauled you back over to see the judge."

Overton batted his eyes in disbelief. "Jake Byrns said that?"

"Damn sure did. 'Course, he only lemme bring in a half quart. Said it wouldn't be fittin' for you fellers to show up in court ossified." Hungate laughed and sloshed the whiskey around in the amber bottle. "Don't worry none, though. This here's powerful medicine. Told the barkeep I wanted the stuff with the live snake in it."

"Well, hand it over," Overton demanded. "You keep runnin' your tongue and he's liable to have a change of heart."

Hungate thrust the bottle out, and the old man tilted it up between the bars and gulped a healthy slug. He waited a moment, shuddering as the whiskey hit bottom, then smacked his lips in a rubbery smile.

"Goddamned if that don't beat the slop they fed us for breakfast."

Colter took the bottle next and helped himself to a generous drink. The fiery liquid seared down through his gullet and just for an instant left him short of breath. He sucked wind, filling his lungs, and his words came out in a hoarse rattle. "Em, I think maybe you was tellin' the truth. That stuff'll pickle your gizzard if you don't watch it."

"Told you, didn't I? Nothin' but the best." Hungate pulled the bottle away and handed it to the old man. Turning slightly, he leaned into the bars with his shoulder, placing his back to the deputy. Under the gurgle of the bottle his voice came in a soft whisper. "Buck, keep your eye on that peckerhead behind me. Lemme know if he starts actin' suspicious. Pass that bottle back and forth and start horsin' around while I'm talkin'."

Overton picked up the cue and let go with a blustery fart. "Christ A'mighty! Put a match to me and I'd go up at both ends."

They all busted out laughing, and as the bottle changed hands Hungate began slipping in comments between the running banter. His tone was terse and low, and filled with a sense of urgency that was unmistakable.

"They're gonna string you fellers up by the balls. Wash Sealy got crocked last night and was braggin' all over town that you're gonna get thirty years. Said he got it straight from the horse's mouth. Way I read it, that means Covington."

"Woooiieee!" Colter snorted. "That is the goddamnedest drinkin' liquor I ever got hold of. Bet it'd even cure freckles."

"Talk around town is that the Association got to the jury and that shitfaced judge. They mean to make believers out of folks by puttin' you away real permanent like."

"Sonovabitch, Buck!" The old man made a grab for the bottle. "You gonna hog that whiskey all for yourself? Have a little respect for your elders."

"What about Sample?" Colter swiped at his mustache, talking behind his hand as Overton slurped whiskey. "You been able to talk to him?"

"Saw him just before I come in here. Says he's gonna start the appeal the minute you're sentenced."

"How long'll it take?"

"He don't know for sure. Six months. A year. Maybe longer."

"Boys, lemme tell you what's a fact." Overton sprinkled a little whiskey on his fingertips and scrubbed his teeth. "This bein' throwed in the hoosegow ain't half as bad as it's cracked up to be. No sireee! Man might even get to where he'd like it."

"So we're gonna be bustin' rocks while he birddogs the courts?"

Hungate dipped his chin in a nod. "That's what she boils down to."

"Johnson!"

Jake Byrns's shout floated in from the front of the jail. The deputy stiffened and cast a doubtful look back at the prisoners. Then he shrugged and disappeared into the office, slamming the door behind him.

Hungate patted his empty holster. "They pulled my fangs before I come in, so I guess they figure I'm harmless."

"Jesus Christ," Overton groaned. "Thirty years. It just don't seem possible."

"Listen, Ed, I don't know about you," Colter rasped, "but I'm not servin' one year, much less thirty. First chance I get, I'm bustin' out and makin' tracks."

"That's the ticket!" Hungate chortled. "Goddamn, I knew you wouldn't take it layin' down. Just knew it."

"What the hell're you talkin' about, Em?"

"Lemme give it to you fast, before that peckerhead gets back in here. I figured you'd come up spittin' nails, so I've had myself a busy mornin'. Now, there's a livery stable catty-corner across the street, between here and the courthouse. I got three horses saddled and waitin'. All you fellers has to do is trick your guards inside when they take you back to court. Then we're off and runnin'."

"No dice," Colter snapped. "You're in the clear, and we're gonna keep it that way."

"Aw, hell, Buck, I ain't got time to argue with you. Play it any way you want. Only make it work, 'cause you mightn't get a second chance."

Colter turned and regarded the old man through the bars. "What d'you say, Ed? You with me?"

Overton couldn't hold his gaze. "Comes hard admittin' it, 'specially after all that fancy talkin' I did, but I ain't got the craw for it. I'm just too goddamned old to hit the owlhoot." He glanced back with a hang-dog expression. "Reckon I'd best take my chances with Sample and the courts. I'll help you out, though. Whatever way you say."

Colter reached through the bars and squeezed his arm. "I'm obliged, but you're better off to stay clean. When I make my play you just hit the dirt and wait'll the smoke clears."

The door banged open and Deputy Johnson entered the cellblock.

"Awright, mister. Visitin' time's over. Make it fast."

Hungate gave them a big wink and turned away. "See you boys in church."

The old man waved and let out a braying laugh. Then he tilted the bottle toward the ceiling and drained it in one long chug.

Overton lurched drunkenly, humming some tuneless ditty to himself as they angled across the street. The prisoners were shackled together by the wrist, and Colter had all he could do to keep the old man upright. Johnson tagged along behind with a shotgun nestled in the crook of his arm, his face pinched in a tight scowl.

"Sheriff's gonna raise billy hell when he sees that old goat drunk. You shouldn't have let him drink what he did. No call for it."

Colter said nothing, but Overton burped and rolled his eyes. "Gotta piss."

"Keep movin', goddammit." Johnson gave them a nudge with the shotgun.

Overton bulled to a halt. "Ain't movin' 'nother step more. Gotta piss."

"Sonovabitch!" Johnson exploded. "Why didn't you do it before we left the jail?"

"Gotta piss." Overton started fumbling at his pants.

"Not out in broad daylight, you stupid bastard." The deputy's eyes flitted nervously up and down the street.

Colter smiled. "Why don't you run ask Byrns what to do?"

" 'Cause he's already up to the courthouse, and you goddamn well know it."

"So, what's to fret? Get the old man off the street and let him take a leak. It's that or haul him into court soppin' wet."

"Shit fire!" Johnson saw people staring at them, and it suddenly dawned on him that they were standing in front of the livery stable. "C'mon, we'll take him in there. It ain't no outhouse, but it'll have to do."

When they entered the livery, Hungate waited back in a shadow until the door swung shut. Then he stepped in from behind and thumped Johnson over the head with his pistol. The deputy grunted, driven forward by the blow, and folded limply to the ground.

Colter whirled on him. "Goddammit, Em, I thought I told you to stay clear of this."

"Well, I'm in it now. Quit your jawbonin' and let's make dust."

Hungate located the key in Johnson's vest pocket and unlocked the shackles. Moments later Colter had the deputy's gun belt strapped around his waist, and paused to shake the old man's hand.

"Thanks for everything, Ed. Look after yourself."

Big tears welled up in Overton's eyes, and he just nodded. Hungate led two horses forward, and both men scrambled aboard. They stared at the door for a couple of seconds, and Colter finally tugged his hat down tight.

"When we hit the street, go like a bat out of hell. Don't stop for nothin'."

"Let 'er rip. I'll be right on your tail."

Overton shoved the double doors open, and they slammed their spurs clean up to the shank. The horses rocketed toward daylight and took the street at a dead lope. Colter was slightly in the lead, and he reined south, gigging his horse again for good measure. People scattered in every direction and over the rush of wind he heard startled shouts race along ahead of them. As they thundered past the courthouse he caught a glimpse of the sheriff and Sam Lyons framed in the doorway, and saw them claw at their guns.

The faint crackle behind him sounded like firecrackers, but suddenly a slug whizzed by so close he could hear it fry the air. Then a bolt of fire punched him in the side, spraying blood across his shirt, and he doubled forward over the saddlehorn. Ducking low, he glanced back just as Hungate swayed and toppled from his horse. The big man hit the ground flat on his back, slack and unmoving. Colter tasted something sour in his mouth, felt it rising in his throat, and he quickly looked away.

Then he was out of town and racing south. Toward No Man's Land.

TWENTY

Wild Horse Lake lay on the divide between the Beaver and the Cimarron Rivers. It was in the western reaches of No Man's Land, and for centuries the Comanche and Kiowa had used it as a campsite during their fall hunts. But the Indians came here no longer. Nor were there any towns or ranches or farms within a day's ride. Wise men avoided this remote stretch of wilderness, for it was a place where neither God nor law was recognized. Judge Colt ruled supreme at Wild Horse Lake, and, not unlike the kingdom of beasts, a man survived on cunning and nerve and a finely whetted instinct for the jugular. Those who came here were both hunter and hunted. In a very real sense they were predators, yet curiously different from other wild creatures. They preyed on their own kind.

The lake itself was actually a large basin, which caught the spring meltoff, and, somewhat like a deep bowl, served as a reservoir for the thundershowers that came infrequently to the plains. Above the basin, sweeping away on all sides, was a limitless prairie where the grasses grew thick and tall. Wild things came here to feed and water, and throughout the year there was an abundance of game. Late fall saw the emerald grasslands cure out in a tawny ocean of graze, and it was said that not even a blind man need fear hunger along the shores of Wild Horse Lake.

Colter sat under a lone oak tree near the rim of the basin, staring off across the prairie. There was a crisp breeze from the north, and the bare bones of the oak knocked and rattled like a skeleton in a high wind. Though he could see for miles in every direction, he was neither watchful nor alert. Wild Horse Lake was a haven for killers and rustlers and every stripe of outlaw known to man. A sanctuary where those who rode the owlhoot could retreat with no fear of pursuit. Not even U.S. Marshals dared venture into this isolated stronghold, for it was common knowledge that, while a lawman might ride in, he would never ride out. A man on the dodge could find no safer place. Whatever his crime, he found immunity here from the laws of both God and man. His fellow predators might kill him, often for the sheer sport of it, a diversion from the boredom and monotony. But in the scheme of things at Wild Horse Lake, men who wore a star simply ceased to exist.

Less than a fortnight back, Colter would have scoffed at the notion of taking refuge in this trackless wilderness. Though its location was known, and easy enough to find, honest men steered clear of it with the same dread as peace officers. Now he thanked whatever gods watched over outlaws that such a place existed. But for Wild Horse Lake, he would be dead, or on his way to prison. And in his mind there was small distinction between the two.

After eluding the posse that dogged his tracks from Meade, he had turned west along the Cimarron. Three days later, gaunt and weak from loss of blood, he had ridden into the basin. According to Dave Shouse, the bank robber who took him under his wing, he had been feverish and out of his head the better part of two days. Colter remembered nothing of this, and only snatches of the grueling ride westward. He recalled awakening one morning with a stiffness in his side and finding that someone had patched him up as neatly as any cowtown quack. The wound throbbed a good deal, and made walking uncomfortable, but it wasn't serious. Shouse, who had performed the repair job, laughed and said that if a man had to get himself shot, it was the best way. Dusted on both sides. In and out. No bones shattered, and the vitals untouched. Hardly worse than getting bit by a yellowjacket.

Colter figured he had come out of it pretty lucky, all things considered, and accepted the offer to share a dugout with Shouse and his gang. Over the next couple of days he met most of the outlaws camped around the lake, some thirty in number, all told, and discovered that they weren't as ferocious as he had imagined. They were hard and ruthless, with all the moral conscience of a scorpion, and possessed no qualms whatever about killing anyone who got in their way. But among themselves they shared an easy camaraderie, and generally a man found trouble only when he went looking for it. They accepted a stranger for what he was—or claimed to be—evincing little or no curiosity about his past or where he came from. It was as if he had been born the minute they laid eyes on him, and whatever he chose to reveal of his past life was strictly his own doing. The men of Wild Horse Lake asked few questions.

Shouse observed over coffee one evening that it sometimes reminded him of a game he had played as a child. A kid had only to cross his fingers and shout the magic words "King's X" and no one could bother him. It was the same at Wild Horse Lake. The law wouldn't come within a half day's ride of the basin, and the men who used it as a haven went out of their way to avoid trouble with one another. There was safety in numbers, much as a pack of wolves band together in hard times, and the death of one diminished the chances of all.

Colter wasn't exactly a skeptic, but he was no pilgrim fresh off the train either. The dugouts around the lake housed a motley assortment of characters—whites, halfbreeds, Mexicans, even some renegade Indians—and every one of them looked like he could eat ground glass without blinking an eye. So long as a man played his cards straight and tended his own business, there was little to fear. But if he stepped on the wrong toes, or turned out to be other than what he claimed, chances were he'd wind up buzzard bait in short order. The men who rode the owlhoot trail practiced a code all their own, one as elemental as death itself: Live and let live, or get snuffed out. There was no middle ground at Wild Horse Lake.

Yet, despite the dull ache in his side and the unsavory bunch he found himself among, Colter's thoughts were far from the basin this particular day. The past few nights he had awakened in a cold sweat, jolted by a dream so vivid and real that it was as if he were there, living it over again. Always it was the same. He was bent low in the saddle, spurring his horse savagely, and, try as he might, he couldn't help looking over his shoulder. Then he saw it. Unearthly, somehow spectral, slowed in time and motion like a hawk suspended high in the sky.

Emmet Hungate stiffens in the saddle and flings out his arms. A bright crimson splotch appears on his shirt front just below the breastbone, as if a brilliant cholla flower has suddenly blossomed on his chest. Then his horse simply runs out from under him, and for a moment he sits there, eyes wide with disbelief, held aloft by some nameless, unseen thing. Slowly he floats to earth, as though being lowered gently and with great care, not falling so much as merely settling. The way a tuft of lint sways and drops with motion arrested. At last he strikes the ground in a soft powdery explosion of dust, landing spread-eagled on his back. The misty spray of earth drifts back over him, turning the blossom on his chest to ruby chocolate, and he lies very still. Frozen in time and space and death.

Colter stared out over the buff prairie and again felt the taste of vomit rise in his mouth. Just as it did each night when he awoke from the dream. But, like the dream, the filth clogging his throat was only an illusion, and he saw it for what it was. Something his mind could hide from by day, to be eluded and shunted aside by force of will. Yet a thing which exerted a will all its own by night, surfacing from the muck and self-loathing he kept buried within himself. The Quakers would have called it guilt, and had the Cheyenne had a word for it, doubtless it would have been the same. Not sorrow or grief or mourning. Just guilt.

Emmet Hungate had not been reckless. Nor had he been arrogant or foolish or excessively brave. His single flaw was poor judgment. He had chosen the wrong man to befriend. A man who prized his own freedom so highly that he would jeopardize the lives of others to break clear. Hungate and Overton had both been endangered by the escape. Older, wiser perhaps, Overton had laid back and lived. Hungate had not been as wise. Or lucky. He chose to stick with his friend, from scratch to finish, and had paid for it with his life. The greater tragedy was that his friend could have stopped him—and hadn't.

Thinking about it, Colter wasn't sure that he would ever purge himself of the dream. Not wholly. Perhaps for the rest of his life he would awaken in a cold sweat. Seeing it again. And maybe, when it came down to the crunch, that was the price he had paid for his freedom. A big, overgrown kid named Hungate.

It was a thing he must live with. Like the taste of vomit.

Uncoiling, he came stiffly to his feet and started down the slope. Twilight had settled over the basin, and it suddenly came to him that he had been sitting under the oak tree since early afternoon. Thinking and thinking and thinking. Which seemed to be all he did these days. Perhaps it was as the ancient ones had taught in his youth: A man gains wisdom not with years but through recognition of his folly.

Ai! There was truth in that. More than he cared to admit.

When he entered the dugout Dave Shouse and his men were seated on their bedrolls eating. Colter didn't have to ask what was for supper. Antelope and beans. The same thing they'd had every night since he came to the basin. Shouse greeted him around a mouthful of beans, and the gang went on scraping their tin plates while he helped himself to the grub. They had accepted him as a boarder of sorts, if not a member of the clan, and some even believed his tale of being railroaded by the Association. Most didn't care one way or another. He was there, and the law was after him, and that spoke for itself.

Shouse took a swig of coffee and flashed a mouthful of brownish teeth. "Get it all figgered out up there, did you?"

"Some of it." Colter returned the smile. "Guess I still got a ways to go, though."

"That's the way of it, for a fact." Shouse

started rolling a smoke, and a curious stillness settled over the room. " 'Fraid I got some news today that's gonna set you to thinkin' a mite stronger."

"Yeah?" Colter glanced up, aware that the other men were watching him closely. "What's that?"

"One of Charley Nave's boys came back from Beaver City today with a load of supplies." Shouse lit his cigarette and studied it a moment. "Association's put a price on your head. Two thousand dollars. Got reward dodgers plastered all over town."

Colter grunted and felt his belly tighten in little knots. "Bastards don't waste any time, do they?"

"Nope. They got a habit of playin' for keeps." Shouse puffed on his smoke awhile, letting that sink in. "It's not just the law no more, y'know. There's gonna be bounty hunters from all over doggin' your tracks. You oughta think on that a spell."

"Guess you're right. It's sure as hell not gettin' any brighter, is it?"

"Well, depends on how you look at it. Me and the boys've talked it over some, and we'd like to have you with us. Figger you got the stuff to make a good hand."

"Robbin' banks?"

"That's our trade. Pays good, too. Better'n cows."

Things were piling up a bit too fast, and Colter needed time to sort it through. "You gotta have an answer right away?"

"Don't reckon so. Like I said, you think on it a spell."

"I'm obliged for all you've done, Dave. Most likely I'd have cashed in if it wasn't for you. But something like this, I've just got to muddle it through on my own."

"Hell, you would've done the same for me. Don't lose no sleep over it."

"Suppose I let you know in the mornin'?"

"Whatever suits. You figger it out and lemme know."

Shouse ground out his cigarette and poured himself another cup of coffee. The rest of the gang got busy cleaning their plates, and within moments they were back gabbing at one another as if nothing out of the ordinary had taken place.

Shortly after dark, Colter went outside to be alone. It was difficult to think with a room full of men swapping windies and passing the jug around. And this was one night he needed to do some powerful thinking.

The idea that he had a price on his head gave him a queer feeling. It was almost as if Covington and the Association had backed him into a corner. So that he'd have no choice but to turn outlaw. But the prospect of riding with Shouse and robbing banks left him a little queasy. These men lived like animals. Burrowed back in a dirt hole they called home. Hunted, always on the run, never sure from one moment to the next that a lawman or bounty hunter wouldn't put a hole through them. They had the clothes on their backs, a fast and easy life, and most likely, an early grave. Except for an occasional whore, none of them even had a woman he could call his own.

It wasn't much of a life. Not by a damn sight.

Without realizing it, he found himself thinking about Rachel and all their plans. If he rode with Shouse, all that went up the flue. Like so much smoke. But if he went back—gave himself up, let Sample enter the appeal—it could work. There was just an outside chance that he might come out clean after all. Then he grunted and smiled to himself, struck by a sudden thought. It was goddamned sure short odds the other way.

A dose of lead or the end of a rope. Even money, take your pick.

Which, all of a sudden, seemed like a real sucker bet.

TWENTY-ONE

The stranger dismounted in front of the main house and left his horse ground-reined. That there was no hitchrack would have given another man pause, but his manner was one of casual indifference. He simply dropped the reins and began swatting dust from his coat. Out of the corner of his eye he saw a chunky, heavy-shouldered man walking toward him from the corral. The description he'd been given of Covington didn't jibe with what he saw, and by simple deduction he tagged the man as foreman of the Circle C. The bow legs and look of authority made it a near certainty. Purely for his own amusement, he mentally made a wager with himself and went back to dusting his coat.

Wash Sealy halted a few paces off and gave him the fisheye, the slow, unhurried once-over he reserved for strangers who rode in unannounced and perhaps uninvited. The ground-reined horse spoke for itself. This was no city jasper. But the handsome twill coat, and beneath it the fancy gunbelt, told a story all their own. This was no saddletramp either, and from the steady way he returned Sealy's stare, it was many a day since he had worked for thirty a month and found.

The inspection done with, Sealy jerked his thumb back toward the corral. "Hitchrack's over that way. The Colonel don't like horseapples right outside his front door."

"Sounds fair, Mr. Sealy." The stranger smiled, but it lacked either warmth or humor. "Maybe one of your boys could look after that little chore for me."

It was more statement than request, and something in the man's voice warned Sealy to go slow. "I don't seem to recollect the face. We met before?"

"Not just exactly. Chalk it up to an educated guess."

Sealy bristled at the evasion, but again something cautioned him to let it lay. "You got business with the Colonel?"

"In a manner of speakin'. He around?"

"Inside. But he don't like being pestered 'less it's important. Most folks just deal with me."

"I guess most folks would." The smile flicked on and off, like a snake skinning back his teeth. "Whyn't you just tell him he's got a visitor? Name's John Ross."

Sealy blinked. "Don't s'pose that'd be the same as Doc Ross, would it?"

"There's some that calls me that."

"Like in El Paso, maybe? Or Deadwood?"

"I've been there, Mr. Sealy. Among other places."

"So I heard tell." The foreman's mouth twitched in a vagrant smile. "The Colonel expectin' you?"

"Would it matter?"

"Not a whole hell of a lot, I guess."

"Good. You just lead the way and I'll tag along behind. Unless you've got some more questions, Mr. Sealy."

"Nope. Reckon I'll just check the bet to the Colonel."

"That's slick thinkin', Mr. Sealy. Real slick."

Sealy had it figured about the same way. They crossed the porch, went through the door without knocking, and proceeded down a wide hallway. The foreman walked directly to a door at the far end of the hall and cleared his throat as they entered the room. John Covington was seated at a desk, working over some ledgers, and he turned toward them with a look of profound annoyance.

"Dammit, Sealy, don't you understand the King's English? I thought I told you I didn't want to be bothered today."

"Yessir, Colonel, you did for a fact." Sealy seemed acutely aware that the man beside him was enjoying this, watching on with that same sardonic smile. "I just sorta figured this was somethin' you'd wanna handle yourself."

"Another of your mind-boggling dilemmas, I suppose?" Covington turned his glacial frown on the stranger. "Well, sir, you're here and I'm listening. What is it you want?"

"Colonel, I forgot to mention"—Sealy gave him the high sign with a cocked eyebrow—"this here's John Ross."

"Fine. Please be brief, Mr. Ross."

"Ah, Colonel, I don't think you caught my drift. This here Mr. Ross is the one they call Doc Ross. Y'see what I mean?"

Covington stared at him blankly for a moment, then nodded very slowly. "Yes. I believe I do." His gaze shifted to the other man. "I'm still at a bit of a loss, though. What business might we have together, Mr. Ross?"

Ross let the question hang for a few seconds, then smiled. "Colonel, I've been instructed to say to you 'The cow jumped over the moon.' "

John Covington straightened in his chair, rigid as a lodgepole. After a long while he glanced back at the foreman. "Sealy, I won't be needing you. Tend to your men and make sure I'm not disturbed again. Understand?"

Sealy nodded, darting a look at Ross, then turned and walked from the room. When they heard the front door close, Covington seemed to unwind a bit and motioned to a chair beside the desk.

"Have a seat, Mr. Ross." He laid aside his pen, shutting the ledgers, and took a moment to collect his thoughts. At last he turned, hands folded and locked in his lap. "Would you mind telling me who sent you with that message?"

"Cal Hunnicut. Head of the Fort Worth Association."

"Are you aware of the meaning behind the message?"

"I am."

"Just so there won't be any doubt in my mind, suppose you tell me what it means."

Ross pushed his hat to the back of his head and hauled out the makings. "Let's quit beatin' around the bush. Whyn't I just tell you what happened and you figure out for yourself if it's the straight goods?"

Covington remained silent, waiting.

Licking the paper, Ross twisted one end of the cigarette and lit it. He took a long drag and let the smoke sift down through his nose. "Six days ago the council in Denver took a vote and decided you need some help. Not that you botched the deal or anything like that, but his Colter fellow escapin' makes it a dicey proposition. Liable to give sodbusters and a whole bunch of cowhands the wrong idea."

"That's crazy! Don't they know we put a reward on Colter's head?"

"Sure you did. Trouble is, you're sittin' back waitin' on some bounty hunter to do your work for you. The council don't figure that'll cut it. We've got to show people that we take care of our own dirty laundry, and prove to 'em we do it damned fast."

"You mean run Colter to earth?"

"Nothin' else. Until the bastard's tracked down and sproutin' daisies, he's a walkin' testament to the joys of cattle rustlin'. Anybody with a boil on his ass and an itch for easy money will just naturally figure to do the same. Things like that has a way of spreadin'."

"Seems to me the council is making a mountain out of a molehill. He's just one man."

Ross flicked the tip of ash with his little finger. "Colonel, cattle rustlin' is like smallpox. It's contagious. You let one man get away with it and pretty soon you've got a hundred throwin' a long loop. That's what happened in Wyoming. The Association up there let it get out of hand, and before it was over we had to go in with a whole damned army to get things straightened out."

He paused and studied his cigarette. "The council don't mean to let that happen again. Not here. Not anywhere else. That's why they sent me."

Covington steepled his fingers, nodding thoughtfully, and began mentally dissecting the predicament he faced. The International Range Association, formed the previous summer in Denver, had awesome power. Its membership was comprised of Association presidents from across the west, and they had voted into being a seven-man council to govern day-by-day affairs. The council's word was law, backed by economic sanctions stemming from alliances with the railroads and large cattle buyers. The advantages of belonging to the International were far-reaching, but cattlemen from individual states dared not buck the council. To do so would result in a dearth of cattle buyers and a scarcity of railroad cars even if a buyer was found. Stockgrowers had gained enormous protection through formation of the International, but the price had been unwavering obedience to the dictates of the council.

This was Covington's first encounter with the council, and for that he silently damned Buck Colter. Yet the pill he was being forced to swallow had about it certain bittersweet qualities. Through Cal Hunnicut, who occupied a seat on the council, he had learned of an interesting development following the Wyoming rustlers' war. The council had formed a secret organization, headed by a former Pinkerton. Its members were quietly recruited from across the West—former peace officers, bounty hunters, and range detectives—and their names were unknown to all except the head of the council. According to Hunnicut, the organization was referred to in meetings as "the Commission," and its purpose was to put the fear of God in rustlers and obstinate sodbusters. Whatever seemed the most expedient means to that end was a judgment left solely to the man sent by the Commission. The presidents of all state Associations were informed of one fact only—if a man appeared using the proper password, they were to obey his orders explicitly. It was a simple password, easily remembered, and somehow highly fitting.

The cow jumped over the moon.

Covington pursed his lips, mulling it a little further, and decided to try a gambit of his own. Lounging back in his chair, he forced himself to smile. "Mr. Ross, I'm wondering, is it politic for me to ask if you've been sent here by the Commission?"

Ross betrayed not a trace of emotion. But his eyes suddenly took on a queer look, blue and cloudy, like carpenter's chalk. Lifeless as death itself.

"Colonel, there's some things better done than talked about. Just between you and me, a man would be real smart if he tended to his own knittin' and forgot he ever heard that name. Savvy?"

"Couldn't be plainer. But it's not enough. I like to know who I'm working with and what stake he has in my game."

"All you have to know is that I was sent, and that when I got here I whispered the right words in your ear. Just leave the rest to me, and we'll both come out smellin' like roses."

"Meaning I should stifle my curiosity and not ask embarrassing questions."

"Meanin' what you don't know can't hurt you. I was told you're a pretty bright fellow, and when our business is done with I'd sure hate to report back anything to the contrary."

However discreetly couched, Covington recognized the warning rattle. Doc Ross was not a man to be antagonized. Though mild-spoken and slight of build, he was known to have a short fuse and a deadly sting. Over the past decade, serving as a lawman in one guise or another, he had cleaned up El Paso, Deadwood, and several lesser hellholes. It was commonly accepted as fact that he had killed no fewer than eight men, and one enterprising journalist had described him as a miniature version of the Grim Reaper. Another had dubbed him the Widowmaker, and still another called him the Undertaker. Curiously, while each of the names fitted him perfectly, none had stuck. He was known simply as Doc Ross, and except for the most foolhardy, that alone was enough to turn the trick.

Staring at him now, Covington saw that he had everything to lose by defying the man. After all, it wasn't Ross giving the orders, but rather some murky organization called the Commission, and, higher still, the council itself. As a military man, Covington had been instilled with a hidebound belief in the chain of command. Moreover, as a confirmed pragmatist, convinced that the ends justified the means every time, he wasn't about to haggle over the use of hired mercenaries. So far as he could see, it was merely a matter of playing the cards he had been dealt, and a rather good hand at that. Letting his sawed-off manhunter call the shots in a situation where he, personally, had everything to gain and absolutely nothing to lose.

"I believe you've made your point, Mr. Ross." Lacing his hands across his stomach, he settled back with a bland smile. "Perhaps it wouldn't be out of order, though, if I asked how you intend to handle this business. I seem to recall that was the word you used. Business?"

"That's right, Colonel. Strictly business." Ross puffed on his cigarette and peered out through a haze of blue smoke. "Huntin' men is a callin' to some, but to me it's a business, pure and simple."

"Does that mean the council wants Colter sent back to jail?"

"What that means, Colonel, is that the council wants Colter dead." Ross waited a moment, then smiled. "I've been sent here to kill him."

TWENTY-TWO

Dodge City was split down the middle by the Santa Fe tracks. North of the tracks was Front Street, the business district, and off behind that the homes of the town's more substantial citizens. Below the tracks, on the Southside, were hotels, stables, dance halls, gambling dens, and a whole raft of honky-tonks. Former lawmen in Dodge, notably Charlie Bassett and Wyatt Earp, had established the tracks as the Deadline. This was some years back, but the name had endured, and with good reason. Trailhands who wandered over the tracks and attempted to hooraw Front Street generally wound up flat on their backs. Most times they were simply clubbed over the skull with a pistol barrel and carted off to jail, but not infrequently they ended up dead. Below the Deadline, though, anything went. They could pickle themselves in rotgut, chase whores, and fight like dogs if the urge came upon them. Just so they didn't kill any of the townspeople. Local peace officers took a dim view of Texas drovers molesting the residents.

The Southside was roaring and popping when Colter rode into town late that afternoon. Texans thronged the street, fresh off the trail and primed for bear. After some three months of nursing longhorns and eating dust, they were thirsty, horny, and game to tackle anything on two legs. Fights erupted with the regularity of clockwork, and the milling, jostling crowds who filled the saloons and dance halls thought it part of the greatest show on earth. The only ones who displayed even passing concern over the brawling and rowdyism were local peace officers. They weren't especially worried about the Texans killing one another, but they felt a civic responsibility toward the Southside dives. Busted mirrors and smashed furniture weren't to be tolerated.

Colter was banking on the very nature of things to provide a smokescreen for his presence in Dodge. It was the end of the season, and every trailhand in town was making a last-ditch effort at pulling the Southside up by its roots. While it was true that Bill Tilghman, the marshal of Dodge, displayed a churlish attitude about outlaws visiting his town, it stood to reason he would have his hands full in these last hectic days of fighting and whoring. Colter would simply melt into the crowd, another cowhand out to see the elephant. The likelihood of anyone spotting him was slim, and if he kept his nose clean all but nonexistent.

Which would give him time for an enlightening little talk with Sam Lyons. The Dodge City Stockgrowers' pride and joy.

This bold excursion into Dodge was something of a last resort. Less than a week past he had shaken hands with Dave Shouse and his gang of bank robbers and ridden east from Wild Horse Lake. The wound in his side was mending fast, and he had eaten enough good red antelope meat to put him back in fighting trim. Yet, in some way he hadn't quite fathomed, he was no longer the same man. Physically nothing had changed. Perhaps leaner, a bit tougher, but no worse for wear. Somewhere in the back of his head, though, things had changed drastically. The death of Emmet Hungate had affected him in a way that was both profound and puzzling.

Slowly guilt had given way to rage, and with it an understanding at last of the great injustice wrought by the Association. Were Covington and his cronies honest men, Emmet Hungate would still be alive. That they were conniving and petty and crooked was the sole reason he had been shot down. Colter saw now, clearly and without doubt, that it wasn't his bid for freedom which had killed Emmet Hungate. The escape had been merely the last act in a tragic sequence of events over which he'd had no control whatever. It was the Association, riddled with greed and corruption, which had set the chain of events into motion. And it was the Association that had ultimately pulled the trigger. Killed Emmet Hungate.

When Colter rode away from Wild Horse Lake, he took with him a confirmed sense of outrage. The easy-going manner, his willingness to give the other fellow an even break, had been replaced with something cold and remorseless. Not unlike his mother's people, the True People, he had become stoic and dispassionate and hard as stone. The Association had smeared his name, killed his best friend, and sent him running with his tail between his legs. They must be made to pay in kind, and he saw himself now as the instrument of their comeuppance. Still, he was not a savage, wronged and demanding blood retribution. Once more he would try the white man's road. The courts. Attempt to find justice, and a measure of revenge, within the legal machinery which presumably served all men equally.

Roughly tracing the Cimarron eastward, traveling only by night, he made his way to Meade. There, in a stealthy meeting with Harry Sample, he learned that justice was not only blind but a fickle bitch as well. The little lawyer explained ruefully that his escape had wiped out any chance of appealing to a higher court. As a fugitive, a man with a price on his head, his alternatives were limited to bad and worse. He could surrender peaceably, resign himself to serving time, and hope for parole at some future date. It was conceivable that in ten years, with a record of good behavior, a parole board would look with favor on his application. The other choice was perhaps even less promising. He could run, change his name, and with any luck get far enough away to build a new life for himself. California or Oregon Territory, Sample noted, were places where many men had swapped their old identities for a fresh start. It wasn't easily done, for the law was relentless and unforgiving, and the greater likelihood was that he would be hounded for the remainder of his life.

The only good news Sample had to relate concerned Ed Overton. The old man was still in jail, but his appeal was before the Federal District Court in Wichita. His chances for a reversal weren't exactly overwhelming, yet certain technical errors by Judge Ashland made it, at the very least, a sporting proposition. Sample extended no guarantees, but he entertained the firm notion that Overton might just win himself a second trial. Before the year was out, one way or the other, they would know definitely.

Colter slipped out of Meade as quietly as he had come, hopes dashed and more angry than ever. While he flatly rejected any thought of surrender, he had no intention of running. Not yet, anyway. He saw no reason to involve Sample, but as the lawyer talked an idea had begun to form in the back of his head. Risky, even foolhardy perhaps, but one that might just work. It was so simple that he damned himself for overlooking it until now. Sam Lyons was the Association's key witness. But he was also the weak link in their case. If he could be tracked down and persuaded to recant his testimony, the rustling charge would disappear in a puff of smoke. Overton wouldn't even need a new trial. The Association would be left holding the bag and, quite likely, facing a few charges of its own.

That night he rode north toward Dodge.

Luckily, he hit the cowtown in the nick of time. Another couple of days and every Texan in sight would be heading south for the winter.

A lone trailhand, wandering the shuttered dives of the Southside, would have stood out like a sore thumb. As it was, he could move about freely, with little fear of detection, and nail Sam Lyons in his own sweet time. After stabling his horse, he made a few discreet inquiries and learned that Lyons rarely left the Association office until well after dark. That suited Colter perfectly. When he braced the cattle inspector, he had an idea a little privacy would fit the ticket nicely.

With that resolved, and a couple of hours to kill, his mind turned to other matters. While recovering at Wild Horse Lake, he had observed that every man in camp was little short of a walking arsenal. Apparently, an outlaw needed to be well armed, and those who had practiced the trade any length of time made it a practice to have several weapons in reserve. Just in case.

Thinking about it on his ride north from Meade, Colter realized that, as a full-fledged desperado, he was a disgrace to the profession. His personal armament consisted of one slightly battered Colt .45, and that lifted off a hick deputy sheriff. He had no saddlegun, no spare pistol, not even a knife. The wonder of it was that he had made it this far without getting himself killed.

Somewhat sheepishly, he set off in search of a gun shop.

The Texans were out in force, jamming the boardwalk, and it took him a while to thread his way through the crowd. But just south of the tracks he came to a halt outside a small frame building. The sign overhead was plain and neatly lettered.

FREDERICK MANNLICH
GUNSMITH
PISTOLS—RIFLES—SHOTGUN

Colter went through the door and found himself in a regular ordnance depot. The walls were lined with racks of long guns, and a large, double-shelved showcase was filled with pistols of every description. At the rear of the store, stooped over a workbench, he saw a portly, gray-haired old man. Approaching closer, he stopped and waited. The gunsmith was tinkering with the extractor in a Winchester '73 and seemed wholly absorbed in the task.

"Mr. Mannlich?"

"Ya. Vot iss it you vish?"

The heavy Austrian accent threw Colter off stride. Then Mannlich turned, and he was even more dazzled. The gunsmith peered back at him through spectacles so thick and glassy it looked like he'd swiped the eyes off a stuffed bear.

"Vell? Speak up, young man."

Colter quit gawking long enough to get out a few words. "I'd like to buy a gun."

"Goot. Ve make progress. Vhat kind of gun?"

"A people gun." Colter bit his tongue, but it was too late. The old man's queer look still had him rattled. "Y'know, something for protection?"

"Ya, I see. Next question. How bad iss it you need protecting?"

"Just about as bad as anybody you ever run across."

Mannlich studied him like a myopic owl. "How much you vant to spend?"

"All it takes. Just make it the best and lots of it."

The gunsmith hobbled to a wall rack and pulled down a rifle no longer than a Winchester but with a polished stock that extended to the tip of the barrel.

"This iss finest rifle made. I shouldt know. Make it myself."

Colter looked skeptical. "Never saw nothin' like that before."

"Ya. Iss new even in old country." Mannlich snapped the bolt back and slammed it forward, jacking out five dummy shells in a couple of seconds. "See? Bolt action. Shoots fifty-caliber shell vid hunnert ten grains powder. Make nice big hole, und accurate at five hunnert meters—uh—quarter mile. Take my vord. Be smart boy und buy."

The gunsmith next selected a pistol from the showcase and displayed it to Colter. It was smaller than a regular Peacemaker, and considerably lighter in weight. "Iss new also. Colt Thunderer. See? Double action." He pulled the trigger, and the hammer rose and fell. "Iss much faster, und short barrel make it easy to draw."

Colter again looked dubious. "Yeah, but will it stop a man? I mean, it's fast and all that, but it's awful little."

"Not so little. I show you." Mannlich pulled a box of .41-caliber shells from the counter and took out a bullet. Then he opened his jackknife and very carefully notched an X across the face of the lead slug. "Now. Bullet strike and spread apart. Like mushroom. Vot you think—stop man? Ya?"

It was so simple, and lethal, that for a moment Colter was left speechless. At last he looked up and grinned. "Ya! I'll take it."

"Vun more thing. Depends how bad your trouble." Chuckling to himself, the white-thatched old man hauled down what appeared to be a lever-action rifle. When he swung it around, it turned out to be a cannon. "Iss latest shotgun. Winchester ten gauge. Hold five shells, und very fast." He jacked the lever in a dizzying metallic whirr. "Shoots double-ought buckshot. Shell holds nine balls, each size of a thirty-two-caliber bullet. Very nice gun for man who hunts people. Und nicer yet if they outnumber him. Iss goot, nein?"

Colter was too bedazzled to argue. The old man plainly knew his business, and the weapons he'd selected were just the thing to keep a fellow healthy and breathing regular. In short order Mannlich had him fitted out with a gun belt for the Thunderer, boxes of shells for each of the weapons, and saddle boots for the rifle and shotgun. Less than a half-hour after entering the shop, he walked out with a dent in his wallet, armed to the teeth. As he went through the door, the old gunsmith looked up from counting his money and chuckled.

"*Auf wiedersehen*, mein friend. Und goot hunting."

* * *

Shortly after dark, Colter eased through the door of the Association office and closed it softly behind him. Sam Lyons was alone, seated at a desk, running totals in a tally book. The latch clicked, and he looked up, squinting against the glare of the desk lamp. Suddenly his face paled with recognition, and he lurched to his feet, scattering papers across the floor.

"Hold real steady, Lyons." Colter spread his hands, showing them empty. "I'm not here to hurt you."

"What the hell's the meaning of this? Whatcha want?"

"I want some straight talk. And if I don't get it, you're liable to lose a little hide. You're pretty slick with words, so I figure you can just jot me down a confession and sign your John Henry."

"Go back on my testimony, is that what you're saying?"

"You catch on real quick. Now, which way you wanna do it? Peaceable, or with lumps on your head?"

"You're crazy as a loon."

"Don't bet your life on it."

Lyons's eyes flicked to the empty hands and the holstered gun. Then he smiled. "Sonny, you've got it a mite backwards. You're the one that's dead."

The cattle inspector flipped his coat aside and clawed at the hideout gun under his armpit. Colter reacted blindly, out of sheer reflex, jerking the Thunderer and squeezing the trigger in a single, fluid motion. The pistol spat three times before

Lyons cleared leather. His chest and throat spurted bright scarlet fountains, and the top of his head vanished in a frothy pink spray as the third dum-dum caught him at the hairline. The impact drove him back against the wall; then he bounced off and pitched face down on the floor. Colter just stood there a moment, enraged by the man's stupidity. And worse, the loss of a witness.

"Sorry sonovabitch. It wouldn't have hurt you to talk."

Still cursing, he stepped through the door and searched the deserted stockyards. Then he swiftly crossed the tracks, a shadow among shadows, and melted into the night.

TWENTY-THREE

A brisk wind swept down over the plains as the sun settled earthward in a splash of molten gold. Colter buttoned his coat, turning the collar up, and kneed the gelding into the water. They forded the Cimarron near the mouth of Timber Creek and swung southeast across the buff grasslands. This was XL range, and he felt a prickling urgency to be off it and onto safer ground. Chances were the XL riders had already called it a day. Were even then toasting themselves in front of the bunkhouse stove. But luck had treated him unkindly in the past few weeks, and he had the feeling of a man who had taken one chance too many. The sooner he was off this spread—and clear of Association land altogether—the better all around. Still, the first purple haze of darkness was shading the sky, and he calculated things were working out just about as he'd planned. Nightfall should find him nearing the Beaver, and the Goddard homestead.

Looking back, he saw now that the trip to

Dodge had been a pipe dream from start to finish. A desperate gamble that had exploded in his face and left him worse off than before. Lyons likely wouldn't have talked even if he'd been roasted over a slow fire. But hindsight was no better than hind tit. It offered a man little besides a gnawing hunger in his belly and a sense of gloomy frustration.

The fact was, he had killed Sam Lyons. Which, oddly enough, didn't bother him one way or the other. The man could lie his way out of a locked safe—had done so on the witness stand—and killing him was little more than he deserved. Circumstances being what they were, though, the law was sure to call it murder. A man shot three times, without ever clearing leather, could hardly be classed as anything else.

Colter grunted, struck again by the ease and quickness of the act. Lyons was the first man he'd ever killed. Like most cowhands, he had fooled around with a pistol, snapped off shots at rattlers and tin cans. But he'd never before drawn on a man. Something that could shoot back. Strangely, he had found it to be an exhilarating experience. There was no remorse, not even a tinge of guilt. It was just something that needed doing. The way a man would shoot a wolf that turned on him, or a rabid dog. What he remembered most was how time had slowed down, split seconds becoming distinct and separate, as though frozen in motion. He could still feel the gun jump and buck each time he pulled the trigger, and etched in his mind was a sharp image of the slugs splattering Lyons up against the office wall. Once he might have been sickened by the thought, revolted by himself and the act. Yet now there was nothing but a grim sort of satisfaction.

Queer as it seemed, killing a man turned out to be a snap.

Not that the aftermath would be any laughing matter. Though he hadn't been seen leaving the office, the law would piece it together quickly enough. When the Association got wind of Lyons's death, they were almost certain to nominate him for the honors. Which meant he was no longer a penny-ante rustler. He was a killer. In the eyes of the law, a man to be gunned down on sight. Or, at the very least, hanged. New reward dodgers would appear, and this time it would be no holds barred. Wanted dead or alive.

However much it galled him, there was no turning back now. Slowly, step by step, he had been pushed over the line. Surrendering to the law, declaring his innocence, would gain him nothing. Just a short trial and a fast hanging. He had to run and keep on running. Until he found a place where nobody had ever heard of Buck Colter. Like Harry Sample had said, California or Oregon Territory. A new name and a new life. If he was lucky.

The one comfort in the whole sorry mess was that there were no telegraph lines into No Man's Land. It would be some days, maybe even a week, before word of Lyons's death trickled south. By then it wouldn't matter. He would be long gone and damned hard to find. But before he left there were a couple of things that needed tending. Hard as it was to swallow, he first had to tell Rachel good-bye. Then he planned to lay a ghost to rest.

The Pony Soldier leader named Covington.

Darkness had fallen when he reached the creek back of the house, and he felt somehow relieved that it was a starless night. There was small likelihood that the Association was having the Goddards watched, not after all this time, and therefore no reason to expect trouble. All the same, the hair on the back of his neck bristled as he dismounted and tied the gelding to a tree limb. He stood there for a moment, staring off toward the house, oddly unsettled. Everything looked the same as it always had, nothing unnatural or out of the ordinary. But his nerves were gritty and on edge, stretched tight as catgut, and something warned him to go slow. After a long while of squinting into the darkness, and straining to catch any unusual sound, he chalked it up to a case of the willies. Like a kid expecting to find a booger man behind every bush. Joshing himself, he stepped out of the shadows and made a beeline for the back door.

The kitchen was dark but still full of warm, savory odors when he entered the house. A shaft of light filtered in from the parlor, and he could hear the murmur of voices. Mostly female, and lots of them, with an occasional deep growl from the old man. The irony of it struck him, and he couldn't help but smile. Joe Goddard was right back where he'd started. Instead of marrying off a daughter, he seemed doomed to ruling a henhouse full of chattering, bickering females. It wasn't exactly justice, but here lately life had a way of playing dirty pool all the way round.

Sarah Goddard saw him first as he came through the kitchen door, and her hand flew to her mouth. "My God!"

"Evenin', ma'am. Sorry to sneak up on you folks this way."

The room went deathly still, and everyone just sat there, shocked into speechlessness. The old man and the girls gaped at him, unable to move their jaws. Rachel started off the settee, then fell back and burst into tears. She buried her face in her hands, and her shoulders shook convulsively. Colter wasn't quite sure what to do, but the others still hadn't moved, so he crossed quickly to the settee and took a seat beside Rachel. She came into his arms like a small, whimpering child, tears sluicing down over her cheeks in salty rivulets.

"C'mon now, that's not any way to greet a fellow. What happened to that golden girl and all them sunny smiles she used to throw around?"

Rachel snuffed and sniffled and blubbered something unintelligible. Then another wave of sobs racked through her, and she clung to him even tighter.

Joe Goddard finally came out of his stupor and managed to get his tongue untracked. "Son, you ain't seen the half of it. She's been bawlin' and mopin' around ever since"—he faltered, looking uncomfortable, and lifted his hand in a meaningless gesture—"well, y'know, ever since we heard you'd run from the law. Just hold on good and let 'er cry herself out. Won't nothin' else stop her, you can take my word for it."

May and Bertha Lou continued to gawk at him, but the old woman at last got her wits collected. She shot a nervous glance at Rachel and then her eyes came level, almost pleading with him. "Buck, these things we've heard—about the law and all—are they true?"

"Miz Goddard, I don't know what you heard, but most likely it's a fact."

Joe Goddard shushed her, but she ignored him and took a deep breath. "The story in town is that you halfway beat a deputy to death and got that Hungate boy killed helpin' you escape. There's some that says you even joined up with a gang of bandits and took to robbin' for a living."

"Oh, Mama, that's vile!" Rachel stiffened and choked back her tears. "Buck wouldn't do anything like that. You know he wouldn't. It's just a pack of lies. The whole thing. Nothing but lies."

"Child, that's what I'm waiting to hear. Your father and me both. But we have to hear it from Buck. Nobody else."

Colter saw the girls go bug-eyed, watching him breathlessly, and his gaze drifted from the old woman to Goddard and back again. It was like trying to explain a nightmare to someone, when it had never made any sense from the start. He didn't rightly know where to begin.

"Ma'am, I sort of lost track of things the last few weeks, but most of what you've been told is pure hogwash. Emmet got himself killed helpin' me escape, awright, and nobody's sorrier about it than me. But he knew what he was doing, and there wasn't no way I could've stopped him. As for the deputy, he wound up with a knot on his head and some hurt feelin's."

"And these robbers you're supposed to have taken up with?"

"That's just an outright lie, Miz Goddard. I hid out at Wild Horse Lake for a couple of weeks, and some bank robbers was nice enough to share their grub with me. But that's as far as it went."

"See, Mama!" Rachel sniffed and shot the old woman a triumphant look. "What did I tell you?"

Joe Goddard hitched his chair around and leaned forward, elbows across his knees. "Buck, you understand we're only askin' 'cause of you and Rachel bein' betrothed. Hell, boy, there ain't nobody we'd sooner believe than you." He paused and hawked, clearing his throat. "The way you snuck in here, though, I'm obliged to ask you—are you still in dutch with the law?"

Colter started to hedge, then abruptly decided to have done with it. "There's no easy way to tell you this, so I'll just say it straight out. I went to Dodge thinkin' I could get one of the witnesses to clear me of that rustlin' charge. He pulled a gun on me and I had to kill him."

"Great God A'mighty!" Goddard stared at him blankly.

Rachel suddenly quit sniveling and clutched at his hand. "Buck, honey, that was self-defense.

The law can't come after you for protecting yourself."

"They can if you're on the dodge from a prison sentence. Besides, it was just him and me. I've got no way of provin' who drew first."

"What—I don't understand, sugar. If you can't prove it, then how are you going to clear yourself?"

"I guess that's what I'm tryin' to say. Why I came here tonight." Colter fumbled for the right words, trying to make it gentle. "It looks like I'm gonna have to move on. California. Oregon, maybe. I don't know just yet. It'll have to be plenty far from here, though."

Rachel blinked back a tear, and her eyes took on a look of aggrieved bewilderment. "You mean—forever?"

He'd never been much of a liar, but now seemed like a good time to start. "C'mon, you know better'n that. I just meant till I get settled some place and can send for you."

Folding her into his arms, he looked over her head and winked at the old man. "Leastways, if your folks'll stand still for havin' a black sheep in the family."

Goddard exchanged a sharp glance with his wife, motioning her to keep quiet. "Buck, you go on and do whatever you've got to. We'll all be waitin' right here when you get yourself set somewheres."

Everybody in the room knew that Colter was spinning a fairy tale, and among them passed a silent accord to honor his last gesture. Rachel wanted desperately to believe, and if she suspected him, she gave not the slightest indication. She dried her tears, dredged up some of her old vivacity, and began chattering about their new home in a new land with animated spirit. Colter played along, never once giving her cause for doubt or alarm. Soon the family was back to laughing and squabbling good-naturedly among themselves, as if it were just another evening spent with Rachel's beau. Sarah Goddard even brought in a cold supper plate and allowed Colter to eat it in the parlor. He wolfed it down with polite greed, having eaten nothing since early morning, and took care not to spill crumbs on her prized carpet. Before long the clock struck ten, and everyone expressed amazement that time had flown by so quickly. The girls were shooed off to bed, and Colter set about making his good-byes. The old woman gave him a big hug, softly whispering her thanks, and Goddard wrung his hand till it ached. Then they headed for their bedroom and left the young couple to themselves.

Colter felt a keen urge to invite Rachel out to the hayloft, but, under the circumstances, he decided it wouldn't be fitting. Instead, he settled for her walking him to the back door. They stood in the darkened kitchen for a long while, kissing and nuzzling, and it slowly became apparent that she meant to hold him as long as possible. At last, after a long, fevered kiss, he took her shoulders and stepped back. The shaft of light from the parlor outlined her face in a cider-glow, and he gently ran his fingertips over her cheek.

"I never said it before, but I've always loved you a lot."

She kissed the palm of his hand, pressing it to her face. "I knew, Buck. Since that first time down on the creek, I always knew."

He nodded, silent a moment, and the words came hard. "Guess I'd better head out. Got a lot of ground to cover before daylight."

She gave him a quick, intent look. "Come back to me, sugar. Or just send word and I'll come running. Wherever you're at."

Colter's mouth quirked in a smile. "I'll let you know. Just as soon as I can."

He kissed her one last time and pulled away, opening the door. She clutched at him, burying her face against his chest, and for a moment they stood framed in the spill of light from the parlor.

"Hands up! We got you covered!"

The shouted command jolted them for a second, and then Rachel grabbed Colter, tugging him back into the kitchen. But the instant she moved the night came alive with fiery orange muzzle flashes, and Colter heard the snarl of a slug as it whizzed past his head. Rachel uttered a sharp gasp, swaying backward a step, and folded limply at the knees. Colter caught her as she fell, easing her to the floor, and kicked the door shut. Outside the rifles barked in a staccato roar and lead splintered through the door, thunking harmlessly against the far wall. Then, unaccountably, the night went still.

Colter bent over the girl, searching for the wound, and his hand came away from her breast warm and sticky. Her eyes opened, glistening blue in the faint light, and she touched his arm.

"Buck"—she smiled like a hurt child—"sugar."

A small shudder swept over her as life gathered in a last flame, then flickered and died. Simply, almost without effort, it seemed, she was gone.

He stared at her, paralyzed, unable to accept it. Then his throat swelled around a moist lump, and hot tears stung his eyes. She was dead. *Dead*. The word exploded in his brain, and he lurched to his feet. A moment later, crazed with grief and hate and a rage to kill, he burst through the door. The Thunderer appeared in his hand, and he sprayed lead into the darkness. But the night was still and empty and eerily quiet.

The killers had vanished.

TWENTY-FOUR

Late that night Colter reined to a halt in a grove of trees overlooking the Circle C compound. He dismounted, hitched the gelding to a stout limb, and walked to the forward slope of a small knoll. There he squatted down and methodically built himself a smoke. He was well back in the tree-line, out of sight, but he took no chances with the match. Flicking it on his thumbnail, he cupped it in his hands, shielding it from view. Then he doused it with a sharp breath and let it drop to the ground. He pulled hard on the cigarette, and the coal flared golden-orange for an instant. In the faint glow his eyes were peculiar, feverish and alert, yet somehow without life. He sucked the smoke deep into his lungs and began a slow, careful study of the buildings below.

The main house was lighted with but one lamp. Observing it awhile, he decided that it was the parlor. Covington was probably sitting there right now, relaxed and gloating. Congratulating himself on a good night's work. Doubtless looking ahead, planning, working out the next step in his grubby scheme. Some very legal and aboveboard maneuver to take over the Slash O and the Broken Arrow C.

A small smile nudged at the corner of Colter's mouth.

Across the way, near the corral and the tack shed, the bunkhouse glowed with light. Colter regarded it with a deepening scowl, and the muscle in his jaw twitched as he ground his teeth in quiet rage. Laughter and the sound of voices drifted in on a chill breeze, noises that had all the earmarks of a party. The Circle C hands were also celebrating. Swilling rotgut and bragging. Congratulating themselves on the blood money they had earned this night. Covington's own little band of hired killers. Bushwhackers and backshooters. Scum who willingly pulled the trigger for a few extra dollars.

Even on a girl.

Stubbing the cigarette out, he came to his feet and walked back to the horse. He hesitated a moment, undecided, looking from the shotgun to the rifle. Then, somewhere in the back of his head, he heard again the voice of the little gunsmith.

Very nice gun for man who hunts people.

Grunting, he pulled the shotgun from its saddle boot and tucked it under his arm. On the spur of the moment, he rummaged around in his saddlebags, found a handful of shells, and stuffed them into his coat pocket. The gelding craned its head around, watching him, and snorted impatiently. He moved forward, making soft horse talk, and lifted the gelding's head. Gently, like a vagrant summer breeze, he blew warm air into the velvety nostrils. The gelding trembled and suddenly went glassy-eyed, bewitched by this creature who cast spells. Colter smiled and leaned closer, whispering a string of muted, woofing grunts.

"Soon, *ekasunaro*. When the hunt is done."

Stepping away, still talking softly, he turned and walked back to the edge of the treeline. Hunkering down again, he jacked a shell into the chamber of the shotgun and eased the hammer onto halfcock. From his pocket he took another shell and fed it into the magazine under the barrel. Five shots. Spewing out forty-five balls of lead. With the Thunderer in reserve, it should be enough. He chuckled quietly to himself. Perhaps more than enough in a crowded room.

His gaze swept down over the compound, judging time and distance. Calculating. Committing to memory the layout of the buildings—a water trough that offered cover if needed—the doors and windows and porch overhangs. Surprise was the key here. Move fast and take them unawares. Bypass the—

Abruptly his thoughts jarred to a halt, and he grunted with disgust. Jingle-jangle-jingle. If he walked in banging a tin drum it wouldn't be any worse. Leaning forward, he unbuckled his spurs and dropped them to the ground. From now on he must think like a Cheyenne. Forget the ways of the *tibos*. Consider the little things that kept a man alive.

Satisfied, he went back to scrutinizing the

buildings. It could be done swiftly and cleanly if a man thought it through. Bypass the main house, for openers. Covington was only one man, and therefore the smallest risk. Hit the bunkhouse first. Hard and fast and brutally. Wipe them out to a man. After tonight it was less than they deserved. That would leave Covington alone and helpless. Allow time to play cat and mouse. Corner him. Let him die slowly, piece by piece. Aware to the very last instant of why and how he was being killed.

An eye for an eye. One putrid, festered soul in exchange for a long-dead squaw and a murdered young girl. Not the white man's way, perhaps. No courts or judges or juries. But justice all the same. Sweet and savory and final.

Tears welled up in Colter's eyes, and he blinked them back. He could still see her face. Hear her last words. Like a little girl asking him to make the hurt go away. Only there was nothing he could do. No time even to tell her of what he felt, all the things he should have said long ago when their world was filled with laughter and stolen moments along a grassy creek bank. One moment she was there and the next she was gone. Like a golden mockingbird—his golden girl—bright and bubbly and gay. Just snuffed out. Gone.

Then the screams. Sarah Goddard and the girls down on the floor, covered in blood, begging their God to make it not so. To let the dead live again. The old man standing numb, eyes glazed, unable to comprehend. A nightmare brought to the home of innocents. And no way to explain it to them. Or set it right. Just meaningless words. The simple mutterings of a fool who had led his own personal hell to their doorstep. A madman who had let a girl take the bullet meant for him.

Only later, after he'd left them wailing and insensible, did he figure it out. The Association, certain he would turn up there sooner or later, had had someone watching the Goddard place. His instincts had been right after all, and blindly he had ignored them. Someone had been watching him when he entered the house, and had probably ridden for help the minute the door closed. Then, like a double-distilled fool, he had loafed around for almost three hours. Plenty of time for them to gather and wait patiently in the darkness. Until the back door opened.

Now Colter closed that door. Slammed it shut in some dark recess of his mind. A cold, wooden look came over his face, and his pale gray eyes took on the texture of thin ice on a freshly frozen pond. The sorrow and pain he had brought to this place ceased to exist, and the core of his inner self focused on nothing save the men below. He climbed to his feet, hefting the shotgun, and started down the knoll. With the first step he was no longer the hunted white man, Buck Colter. His thoughts reverted to the Cheyenne tongue, and he became *biraxdeta*.

The hunter.

Sticking to the shadows, he came down off the knoll and crept along a narrow arroyo that snaked northward behind the house. Waiting a moment, he surveyed the rear windows, satisfying himself that the rooms were dark and empty. Still alert to any sound or movement, he scrambled out of the defile and took off in a shuffling dogtrot, skirting the side of the house. At the front of the building he stopped, peered cautiously around the corner and scanned the compound. The party in the bunkhouse was still going full blast, and there was no one in sight. Waiting for a fresh burst of laughter, he sprinted across the open ground, skidding to a halt beside the tack shed. There he took several deep breaths, letting his heartbeat settle to a slow, rhythmic pace. At last, hand steady, icy calm restored, he quit the shadows.

Quiet as woodsmoke, without a whisper of sound, he catfooted past the shed. The noise grew louder as he neared the bunkhouse, and he could now separate voices and words from the general clamor. Gaining the corner of the building, he flattened himself against the wall and inched toward the window. Light filtered through the glass, casting a soft glow on the earth, and a few steps farther on was the door. He removed his hat, holding it at his side, and then, with the utmost care, edged one eye around the window casement.

There were seven men in the room. Four playing poker at a table to the left of the entrance. Two more seated in front of a potbellied stove, their backs to the door, sharing a bottle. The last man was stretched out in his bunk, directly across from the poker table, swigging from a tin cup. One of the men playing cards, seated farthest away from the door, was Wash Sealy. Behind him was another door, apparently leading to the foreman's private quarters.

Colter jerked his head back, shutting his eyes tight, and burned every detail of the room into his mind. The corner of his mouth lifted in a crooked smile, and his eyes opened. It was still risky, but the unsuspecting fools had made it easy for him. As easy as seven against one could ever be. He crammed his hat on his head and came off the wall. Then he went stock still, listening. Someone inside was talking, gloating, and the words chilled his blood.

"Whatcha think, Slim? You saw her better'n the rest of us."

"Beats me. I just know I was slingin' lead as fast as I could. Wasn't hardly time to stop and count noses."

Another voice chimed in. "Red, what difference does it make anyhow? I don't see no reason to get your bowels in an uproar."

"I ain't got nothin' in an uproar. I'm just askin', that's all. Killin' women ain't exactly my style."

"Who says we killed her?"

"Judas Priest! You gone loony or somethin'? We must've put fifty shots through that door."

"Well, who gives a shit?" This came from one of the men near the stove. "Pike, lemme tell you what's the God's own truth. Sodbusters is sodbusters. And nobody's gonna bat an eye 'cause this one was a gal."

"That's for damn sure," Slim agreed. " 'Specially the Colonel. Hell, I'll bet him and Ross was standin' around toastin' one another like a couple of politicians."

"Now there's one man I don't cotton to," Red grumbled. "Sonovabitch looks like he sleeps on broken glass and pisses ice water."

Wash Sealy laughed. "If I was you, I wouldn't go around bad-mouthin' the likes of Doc Ross. He ain't so big, but he's sudden. Real sudden."

"Goddamn if that's not a fact!" Pike howled. "Right after he told Colter to get 'em up, that little runt let fly, and I'll betcha he had his Winchester plumb empty 'fore I ever rightly got started."

"Yeah, but who needs him? We could've done that job easy as pie. Lemme ask you somethin', Wash. How come the Colonel brought him in on this deal, anyhow?"

"Tell you the truth, I ain't so sure it was the Colonel's idea. I got a hunch somebody sent Ross here. Couple of times I even got the feelin' he was the one givin' the Colonel orders."

"What d'you mean, somebody *sent* him here?"

"Somebody like the big dogs in Denver," Sealy observed. "Looks to me like any time they say frog, the Colonel squats. And I'll lay you good odds it was them that sent Ross."

"Well, you can't fault him," Slim insisted. "Little bastard got Colter, didn't he?"

Pike laughed. "Yeah, I'll bet him and the Colonel are back in town hangin' one on. Jesus, that kid gave the boss a real fit there for a while. Never saw nothin' like it."

"Pike, you ain't got the brains of a pissant." Sealy snorted, and there was the sound of a bottle striking the rim of a tin cup. "Only reason the Colonel stayed in town was to give himself an alibi. When word gets out about the shootin', there'll be all kinds of people that can swear they saw him in the Yellow Snake the whole night."

Colter stiffened and glanced back at the house. It was empty! Covington had been in town all the time. Cursing, he turned his ear again to the men in the bunkhouse. A new name had surfaced—someone called Ross—and he wanted to hear more of the man.

Red was talking. "What about the runt? Who's gonna cover for him?"

"Ross? Is that who you're talkin' about?" Sealy asked. "Christ, he don't need no alibi. There's nobody stupid enough to tangle with Doc Ross. Lawman or otherwise."

"Say, y'know somethin' that's been puzzlin' me?" There was a moment's silence, and everybody turned to look at one of the men in front of the stove. "Ever since we rode off I been wonderin' if Colter was gettin' in that little gal's pants."

"Sure he was, stupid. Them sodbuster women put out for anything that stands on its hind legs. Even an idjit knows that."

"Well, he ain't no more!" Pike whooped. "Not with a pecker full of holes."

A burst of laughter erupted from inside, and someone pounded the table in a fit of glee. After a while the laughter subsided, and there was the sound of a chair being scraped back. Then Wash Sealy spoke.

"I don't know about you boys, but I'm gonna

get some shut-eye. We still got a spread to run, and sunup comes awful early. See you in the mornin'."

Colter waited, listening for the inner door to shut; then he moved. Stooping low, he ducked under the window and quietly walked to the bunkhouse door. He drew a deep breath, thumbed the hammer back on the shotgun, and aimed a savage kick at the latch. The door burst open with a splintering groan, and he charged through. The bore of the shotgun looked like a mine shaft in the crowded room, and everyone froze as he leveled down and clamped the butt tightly against his hip.

Disbelief permeated the bunkhouse. The men stared at him as if they were seeing a ghost—the risen dead—and he gave them no time to recover from their shock. Hours ago he had decided that this was to be an execution, not a fair fight. Pivoting to the left, he pumped two fast shots into the men seated at the card table. Buckshot sizzled across the room, like a fiery hailstorm, and the three men were blown away from the table in a bloody tangle of flailing arms and thrashing legs. Cranking the lever, he turned and triggered a round into the two men in front of the stove. The load struck them broadside, not five feet away, just as they came out of their chairs. They reeled drunkenly, slammed into the red-hot stove, and pitched to the floor. Their clothes were singed and smoking, and one man had been disembowled as neatly as a gutted hog. Colter worked the lever and wheeled toward the bunk at the far side of the room. Terror-stricken, bleating little sheeplike whimpers, the man there clawed frantically at a holstered gun on the bunk post. Colter fired, and the man's head vanished in a cloud of skull fragments and globs of frothy brain matter.

The door at the far end of the room wrenched open, and Colter crouched, levering the last shell into the chamber. Wash Scaly was framed in the doorway, gun in hand, eyes wide and distended as he glimpsed the carnage. Then his gaze fell on Colter, and his mouth worked in silent horror.

"Glad you could join us, Wash." Colter smiled and swung the shotgun a notch higher. "I saved one for you."

The blast caught Sealy in the chest, shredding him with a plate-sized pattern of lead, and he hurtled backward. His bare feet flapped the air, and, like some grotesque, lumpy scarecrow, he settled to the floor in a puddle of blood.

Colter ejected the spent shell and calmly reloaded the shotgun. All the while his eyes moved about the room, oblivious to the entrails and the splattered gore and the stench of death. Satisfied that the seven men were dead, he cradled the shotgun in the crook of his arm and methodically built himself a smoke. Almost as if he were removed from it, abstracted somehow, he saw that his hand was steady as a rock when he struck the match.

Ai! Grunting to himself, he turned and walked from the bunkhouse.

TWENTY-FIVE

Colter left the gelding behind the sod schoolhouse and walked to the front of the building. This late at night, Benton was generally pretty quiet, and the town appeared just about as he'd expected. Light sprinkled out in fuzzy beams from the Yellow Snake and Dix's, but otherwise the street was black as a tar barrel. Horses lined the hitchracks in front of both saloons, standing hipshot and drowsy in tight little bunches. A quick count indicated that the Yellow Snake had pulled the most trade tonight. Which stood to reason. Covington and his cronies were likely hoisting a few in honor of the occasion. Providing themselves with an iron-clad alibi. Just in case some U.S. Marshal ever took a notion to ask around about the night's dirty work.

Chances of that were slim, though. So remote that Colter hardly gave it a second thought. Unless someone filed a complaint, lawmen generally stayed the hell out of No Man's Land. Tonight's gathering of buzzards at the Yellow

Snake was strictly for show. A theatrical of sorts. Something to convince the townspeople, and through them the law, that Benton's leading citizen was pure as the driven snow. All of which merely reaffirmed in Colter's mind the need to finish this in his own way.

His first thought had been to waylay Covington on the river trail. Simply wait at some dark spot and kill the sorry bastard as he rode back to the Circle C. But, upon closer scrutiny, Colter had discarded the idea and headed straight for town. Something new had been added to the game—a man named Ross. Apparently the one who had organized and led the ambush at Goddard's place. There was an outside chance that Ross wouldn't return to the ranch with the Colonel. And from what he'd overheard at the bunkhouse window, Colter suspected that one needed killing as bad as the other.

The name Wash Sealy had used—Doc Ross—was familiar somehow. But Colter couldn't place it just exactly, and he'd wasted little time puzzling over it. His thoughts dwelled instead on what had been said about Ross. Plainly the man had been sent here by the International Association, and it seemed equally clear that he was a hired gun. Not a bounty hunter, but something worse: a paid killer.

Colter was scarcely surprised. Big cattle outfits had been using hired guns for years, and it figured that the Association would stick with accepted practice. Especially one that had proved itself in range wars and water disputes throughout the West. Like as not, the International in

Denver kept several of these gun-hawks on the payroll. Men whose stock in trade was killing, and under whatever guise, earned their keep performing the Association's dirty work. It made sense, and from the snatches of conversation he'd overheard outside the bunkhouse, this Doc Ross was just such a man.

What bothered Colter most was not that he had to go up against a hired gun. The fact that Ross had been instrumental in Rachel's death automatically marked him for killing. The same as Covington and the others. Colter's singlemost worry was that the man might kill him before he could get to Covington. Which meant that Ross had to be taken out first, and decisively. Without any pretense of an even break. Nonsense like that was risky enough at the best of times, and against a hired killer it was just plain stupid. Somehow he had to get the drop on Ross and eliminate him the fastest way possible. That people would consider it less than sporting seemed unimportant. The man had casually performed murder—killing an innocent young girl who had never harmed anyone—and Colter had no qualms whatever about killing Ross.

But first he had to catch him with his pants down. And from what Wash Sealy had said, that would be no small chore in itself.

Thinking about it now, Colter kept to the shadows of the schoolhouse and carefully examined the Yellow Snake. To burst through the front door would be nothing short of suicide. Judging from the horses outside, there were upward of a dozen men in the saloon. Most of them men he had no wish to kill, despite their link to the Association. The situation called for surprise—the same as he'd pulled off at the bunkhouse earlier—and that put a quietus of sorts on the front door. But if he came through the back door. Took them from behind.

The more he weighed it, the better it sounded. With a little luck, and a damn good bluff, it might just work. Things being what they were, he wasn't exactly in a spot to pick and choose anyhow.

It had to work.

Satisfied it was the best he could manage, he retraced his steps to the gelding. There he collected the shotgun, and, after checking its loads, quartered off toward the rear of the business district. Several houses sat back away from the stores, but it was late and there were no lights showing. All the same, he stuck to the deeper shadows, hugging the rear walls of the buildings. If anyone detected him now, they wouldn't ask questions. Not at this time of night, with him skulking along in the dark. It would strictly be a matter of whose ticket got punched first.

Suddenly something loomed up out of the night, moving toward him in a pounding rush. He spun about, dropping into a crouch, and thumbed the hammer back on the shotgun. Just as his finger curled around the trigger, he caught himself and held off. It was a gut reaction, sheer instinct, warning him not to risk a shot in the dark. A moment later something furry and full of wiggles brushed up against his leg. Lean and slobbery, all tongue and sticky kisses, it was a lonesome dog making its nightly rounds. Colter's nerve ends jangled like chain lightning, and he slowly became aware that he was holding his breath. Then the tightness across his chest slacked off, and he hissed at the dog.

"Get outta here, you mangy devil! Go on—git!"

The dog streaked off into the darkness, headed in a beeline for the distant houses. Colter waited a moment, letting his nerves settle down, then struck out again. The smell of urine and puddled earth became stronger with each step, and he knew it wasn't far now. The back door of the Yellow Snake was generally left open, so the customers could have a leak when the urge took them, and he was banking on tonight being no different from any other. A few steps farther and he felt the mushy ground, soft and damp beneath his boots. Groping blindly, he ran his fingers over the roughhewn door, working strictly by feel. Then he had hold of the latch—drew a deep breath—and slowly lifted the pegged bar.

It was unlocked.

Colter eased through the door and closed it softly behind him. The storeroom was dark, crowded with a jumble of kegs and crates, but a spill of light sifted through the door leading to the saloon. Beyond the entrance he heard the low murmur of voices, and he stood listening a moment, letting his eyes adjust to the dim light. After his vision cleared he began working his way across the room, weaving cautiously between packing cases, barrels, and an accumulation of litter covering the floor. Edging closer to the door, he dropped to one knee and took a quick peek into the saloon. It was enough, and he jerked his head back before anyone could spot him.

Smiling, he grunted softly to himself. The bastards couldn't have arranged it better if he'd laid it out himself. Steady now, alert but calm, he eared the hammer back on the shotgun and stepped through the door.

At first no one saw him. Covington was seated at a table off to the left, playing poker with Sim Hardesty of the Box T and several other ranchers. Nearby another game was in progress, and Alex McCord, foreman of the XL, sat facing the door. Doc Ross stood at the bar, a solitary drinker, nursing a glass of whiskey. George Parker, owner and head barkeep, was hunched over the counter, eyes nodding like a sleepy vulture. McCord happened to glance up, and the cards fluttered from his hand as his face drained of color.

"Freeze! First man that moves is dead."

Colter's barked command brought everything in the room to a halt, and a startled hush fell over the men. Covington and the other cattlemen stared at him in shocked disbelief, hardly able to credit their eyes. Ross betrayed no emotion whatever. He merely turned his head and looked at Colter, as if gauging a mistake that must again be dealt with in some manner.

"Everybody keep your hands in sight and you won't get hurt." Colter waggled the muzzle of the shotgun, indicating the bar and the nearest poker table. "This is strictly personal. Between me and the Colonel and his hired gun. Anybody butts in will just have to take his chances."

Covington's features were sallow, almost waxen, but he managed to get hold of himself. "Colter, you'll never get away with this. I suggest you put that gun down and we can discuss our differences like reasonable men."

"Don't be in a rush, Colonel. I'm comin' to you. Right after I tend to your gunslick." His gaze shifted back to the bar. "Just so there won't be any mistakes—you're Ross, aren't you?"

Ross nodded and looked away, studying his whiskey glass. "Seems like you got more lives'n a cat."

"You ought to know."

"Mebbe. What's your business with me?"

"Time to pay up. You killed a girl tonight, and I'm here to collect."

"What are you talking about?" Covington jerked erect, halfway out of his chair, then settled back as the shotgun flicked in his direction. "What's this about a girl?"

"You mean Ross forgot to mention that, Colonel?" Colter's eyes bored into the gunman. "Go ahead, Ross, tell 'em about Rachel Goddard."

Ross sipped at his whiskey and slowly set the glass on the bar. "You'll have a hard time provin' that."

"I got all the proof I need. The Colonel's men couldn't hardly talk about nothing else."

A deadened silence fell over the saloon, and the men at the tables turned to stare at Ross. After a moment he shrugged, and a sardonic expression crept over his face. "You expect me to go up against a scattergun? That's not givin' a man much of a chance."

"More chance than you gave the girl."

"What if I won't draw?"

"Suit yourself. You're dead either way."

"Now if you didn't have that cannon pointed—"

Ross spun, crouching, his hand a blurred motion. The movements were executed so smoothly, faster than the eye could follow, that Colter had time only to react. He pulled the trigger a mere instant after Ross cleared leather. The shotgun roared flame, and Ross staggered backward as if struck by a thunderbolt. His crotch blossomed red as the buckshot opened a gaping hole in his lower belly and blood splashed down over his pants. Then, as if his backbone had been snatched clean, he simply collapsed and crashed to the floor. His legs twitched convulsively, and a stench spread over the room as his bowels voided. After a moment his eyes rolled back in the sockets, and he lay still.

The men seated at the tables stared on, spellbound, unable to pull their eyes away from the gory, blood-splattered corpse. By now Colter had become insensitive to the shotgun's handiwork, and he scarcely gave the body a second glance. Walking forward, he stopped at the end of the bar.

"You're next, Covington."

His words snapped the men out of their trance, and they turned toward him. Covington's face went ashen, and it was a moment before he could speak. "You're crazy. No sane man just goes around murdering people."

Colter's laugh was scratchy, abrasive, like a match being struck. "You got a lot of room to talk, don't you?"

"Before God, I knew nothing about the girl. Nothing."

"What about Sand Creek, Colonel? Remember that?"

Covington shook his head numbly. "I don't understand."

"Like hell you don't. I was there, Colonel. I saw it. What happened tonight wasn't no different from what you did to them women and children at Sand Creek. Try tellin' me that wasn't murder."

"I—you're Indian?" Covington's look was wide-eyed, incredulous.

"What I am don't matter. I just wanted you to know why I'm gonna kill you. Now that you do, there's no sense wastin' words."

Colter laid the shotgun on the bar, within easy reach. Nothing was said, but the other men understood perfectly. Anyone who tried to interfere would get a dose of buckshot for his trouble.

"Covington, I'm gonna give you a better chance than you ever gave anybody else." With his left hand Colter extracted a shell from his cartridge belt. "You've got a pistol. Use it before this hits the floor, or I'll kill you where you stand."

He tossed the shell high in the air, and Covington's gaze flicked upward as it scribed an arc near the ceiling. When it started down, the cattleman came alive in a spastic frenzy, clawing frantically at the gun on his hip. Colter waited, allowing him to clear the holster, then brought the Thunderer level and fired. A bright red dot appeared above Covington's belt buckle, and before he could fall Colter stitched three more holes up his shirt front. The last slug caught him in the throat, and as the dum-dum mushroomed, his Adam's apple exploded in a spurting, crimsoned mist. The impact slammed him back against the wall, and he hung there a moment, suspended in death. Then he slumped forward and slid to the floor in a sudden, bloody heap.

Colter holstered the Thunderer and took up the shotgun. Backing slowly away, he halted at the entrance to the storeroom and let his cold glare rove across the seated cattlemen. "You're as sorry a bunch of bastards as ever lived. But if you've got any sense, you won't forget tonight. This is what happens when you push a man to the wall. Think about it next time you start gettin' greedy."

They stared back at him, paralyzed with fear, and after what seemed a lifetime his glance shifted to Alex McCord. "Alex, I'd be obliged if you told folks the truth of what happened here. All I done was give a couple of killers some of their own medicine. Maybe it wasn't legal, but it's likely the only kind of justice that would've turned the trick."

McCord merely nodded, unable to hold the icy stare, and looked down at the table. When he glanced up, Colter was gone. A moment later the back door slammed shut, and an eerie stillness settled over the saloon. The quiet of a charnel house when the slaughter is done.

The Dipper had rocked far down in the sky as Colter rode away from the clearing on Cottonwood Creek. Behind him, the cabin he had built for Rachel blazed fiercely in the night. Like the girl with golden hair and laughing blue eyes, the dream was dead. The ash inside him was cold and without feeling, and he didn't look back. But he found a certain grim satisfaction in the knowledge that no stranger would ever live in the cabin. The flames seemed queerly symbolic in his mind. A fitting tribute to what once was and all that might have been. Rachel would have approved.

He reined the gelding upstream and rode north toward the river trail. By sunrise he would be nearing the Cimarron, and in a few days he would be safe again at Wild Horse Lake. Time enough then to think of what lay ahead. Just now he had his hands full with what lay behind.

Looking back, he was struck by the ironic twist his life had taken. Six years he had followed the white man's road. Suppressing the ways and thoughts and ancient beliefs of the True People. The Cheyenne. Now he rode alone—neither Indian nor white—committed to a path all his own. A man answerable only to himself and the will to endure.

Yet he would never truly be alone. Where life has no value, death often has a price, and his backtrail would be crowded with those eager to bring him down. Bounty hunters. Lawmen. The Association's hired killers. There would be no scarcity of men who preyed on their own kind for a price. After this night he was marked an outlaw for all the days of his life.

A renegade with no salvation but his gun.

Perhaps that was the most ironic twist of all. Within the space of a few days he had killed ten men. Deliberately and coldly and without remorse. For someone who had never before fired a gun in anger, it had about it a dreamlike quality. As if it were happening to some other man far removed in time and distance. But it was no dream. He had snuffed out ten lives in a bloodletting that wouldn't soon be forgotten.

The thought gave him a moment of wry amusement. Ed Overton, in particular, wouldn't forget. With all the witnesses dead, the old man was sure to win his freedom in a second trial. Maybe then he would find peace, at last, along the Beaver.

As for himself, Colter harbored few illusions. After the bloodbath in No Man's Land, the Association would hound him to the end of the earth. They had no choice. It was that or eat crow before all the world.

Still, there was a certain intoxication to this thing of being a wanted man. Strangely so, like a jolt of snake-head whiskey on a warm evening. After all, the one being chased could always turn and fight. Whenever it suited him. Anywhere. Anytime.

Colter grunted, chuckling softly to himself,

and feathered the gelding's ribs. *Ai!* It was as the ancient ones had taught in the days of his youth.

Those who tracked the wolf were less hunter than hunted.

pb
3 7/14 N